NANTUCKET DAYBREAK

NANTUCKET DAYBREAK

by James Sulzer

WALKER AND COMPANY
NEW YORK

Library of Congress Cataloging-in-Publication Data

Sulzer, James.
  Nantucket daybreak.

  I. Title.
PS3569.U37N3   1987   813'.54   87-37271
ISBN 0-8027-1013-1

First published in the United States of America in 1988 by the Walker Publishing Company, Inc.

Published simultaneously in Canada by Thomas Allen & Son, Canada, Limited, Markham, Ontario.

Printed in the United States of America

10 9 8 7 6 5 4 3 2 1

for Barbara

NANTUCKET DAYBREAK

They are a pretty sight from a distance, the scallop boats, as they work their way slowly across Nantucket harbor against the slanting rays of November sunlight. The steady rhythm of the work lends an added charm; it seems in harmony with water and wind and sky. Long, taut ropes stretch off into the water from the stern of each boat. At regular intervals, the ropes are hauled in and the attached dredges dumped out. The men and women on the boats seem to move with unhurried grace, like figures from some older, slower time—like the whalers, perhaps, who made Nantucket famous in the early days of America. The boats and the scallopers seem as poetic and pristine as pictures from a maritime history.

But come closer, and you see that survival—not purity, not history, not tradition—motivates the scallopers and their choice of boats. It is as though the great whaling fleet of old were splintered into small, mismatched fragments. The boats are a ragtag collection of old and new, commercial and pleasure, wood and fiberglass, inboard and outboard craft. Some have cabins, most do not; some are freshly painted, most are not. They range in length from twelve to thirty feet. About the only common features are the culling boards, bolted from gunwale to gunwale halfway back in the cockpits, and the square metal frames above.

And while there may be a poetry in the work, it is not leisurely. The scallopers work furiously, often from dawn to dusk, dredging up the bottom of the bay and keeping only the scallops that by law can go to market. They are out six days a week, from November through February; they are forbidden to work on Sundays.

Each boat tows six or eight dredges, each around two feet wide. Well-constructed dredges pick up practically everything: eelgrass, beer bottles, toadfish, flounder, crabs, conchs, mud, pieces of wood, rocks, sand, bricks—and sometimes scallops. Only the healthy adult scallops, two years of age, can be kept. The seed scallops, which are a year old, must be thrown back for another year.

It can take anywhere from two to twenty-five tows to bring in a day's catch of ten bushel boxes of good scallops. This "double limit" (each of the two fishermen per boat is allowed a single limit of five boxes) is then taken into the shanties and given to the openers. The opening is the most tedious part of the whole process, which begins with a ragtag fleet and ends with a blunt metal knife.

The shell of the Nantucket bay scallop is roughly the size of the palm of your hand. It is fan-shaped, with a series of radiated ridges that taper off toward the edges. Ranged along the inside edge of the shell are two rows of eyes, each the size of a pinhead. The eyes are an eerie, phosphorescent blue; while they are sensitive to light, they cannot discern shapes. But no one—fisherman or consumer—is especially interested in these eyes. The bay scallop, even more than its larger cousin the sea scallop, is prized for its other "eye"—the white, firm, plump muscle inside its shell. This is the gourmet food that appears on the tables of fancy restaurants in New York and Boston and Washington. This is what creates a multimillion-dollar cottage industry each year in Martha's Vineyard and Cape Cod and Nantucket, employing high-school dropouts and Harvard graduates alike. But like the legendary Cyclops, after a scallop loses this eye it is worthless. Truckloads of shells and guts are carted off from the shanties each day, to be dumped somewhere far away from people. For there is no smell quite like that of rotting scallop guts—as though to remind everyone that this pure, nutritious food has its roots in the mud and slime at the bottom of the sea.

CHAPTER 1

It was a fair, windy morning in mid-November. The scallop fleet was spread over the harbor; two weeks into the season, most of the jockeying around for position had temporarily subsided and the fishermen had chosen spots that they might work for several weeks. Two boats were within hailing distance of each other in the area known as Horseshed, a spot near the mouth of the harbor famous for its strong tides, large scallops, and messy bottom. (The area was so named because, over a century earlier, a shed for horses had stood on the nearby shore.) Across the bay, the town of Nantucket rose on a long hillside, culminating in the familiar gold dome of South Church.

On one of the boats in the Horseshed, two young men in their middle twenties stood across the culling board from each other. They wore identical yellow oilers and brown waterproof gloves, and both of them were troubled by noses that wouldn't stop running. But there the resemblances ended. Russell O'Grady, the owner and captain of the boat, towered over the culling board at 6 feet 4 inches and 230 pounds. He stood to the stern and was responsible for setting and hauling in the dredges. Under his oilers he wore a dry diving suit—nothing more. When he hung up the diving suit each night after work, it gave off a smell of flesh and scallops that fascinated his year-old son and attracted the interest of the cat. A high-school graduate from Providence, Russell had lived on Nantucket for four years. He had come as part of an off-shore fishing crew and liked it so much he never left.

Kevin White, the mate or crew member, was small and slight. He stood on the bow side of the culling board, and it was his job to sort out the legal scallops and dump them into boxes. Under his oilers he wore underwear shorts, long underwear, a flannel shirt, a pair of lined Oshkosh blue jeans, two sweaters, and a hooded sweatshirt—all new and barely tainted with the odor of scallops. Kevin's hands moved with uncommon grace and dexterity; they were quick and accurate from years of playing the violin. But his eyes were weak; he was continually stopping to clean his thick wire-rimmed glasses. He had majored in music at Harvard and begun graduate work there, but after one year he suddenly gave it up and joined his girlfriend on Nantucket.

Russell's dredges were twenty-four inches across—the maximum allowable size—and with each tow in the Horseshed they filled to bursting with grass and muck and scallops. They were getting about three baskets per tow—a little better than a box. After four tows, Russell and Kevin were halfway through for the day. The four-faced clock on the church tower said noon. Russell was already tired from hauling in the dredges, which weighed over a hundred pounds when full. And he was growing more and more upset by the slowness of his culler. It wasn't that Kevin couldn't move quickly, but he would pick up a scallop and stare at it, as if weighing all the pros and cons before deciding whether it was good or not. So far today, Russell had culled over half the scallops himself, though that was not supposed to be his job.

He had chosen Kevin as his mate by a kind of fluke. He had had an experienced culler all set to go, when her father had a heart attack and she had to leave the island to care for him. That was just a few days before the start of scalloping season. Russell was working on his boat the next day—getting the dredges ready—when Kevin showed up on the dock. Russell had seen Kevin around town and knew he was respected for some sort of accomplishment. They got into conversation, and one thing led to another. Kevin was looking for work, and all the experienced cullers were already spoken for. So Russell decided to give Kevin a chance. Although Kevin's Ivy League background was foreign to him—only one of the O'Grady boys had wanted to go to college—Russell felt a remote affection for it; his own father had gone to Brown. He had assumed that Kevin could do the job. Now he wasn't so sure.

Russell threw out the dredges again and set a new tow, careful to hit the edge of the channel where the grass was thinner. A huge mound of junk and scallops lay heaped on the culling board from the previous tow. Kevin was holding up a large scallop—obviously seed to Russell's experienced eye. Finally, Kevin tossed it in the basket. Russell reached over and tossed it out of the basket and into the water without saying anything. He steered along the edge of the channel, swung the boat around, and came back again from the other direction. Kevin had made a small dent in the corner of the mountain of debris on the board.

"With vigor, Kevin," Russell urged, over the drone of the outboard. "Let's have a little vigor, okay?" Kevin didn't look up, but his face reddened. He started moving faster. In quick succession he knocked five small adults off the culling board, into the water. Russell rolled his eyes but didn't say anything. A muscle twitched nervously in his jaw; sometimes at night Russell ground his teeth in his sleep.

Kevin threw another seed into the basket, and Russell shook his head.

"Remember, shell size has nothing to do with whether or not it's seed," he told Kevin. "Some adults are little; some seed are big. But adults are fatter. Seed tend to be flat, like this one." He held up a large seed for Kevin to see. "And the adults have a growth ring. See? There's no growth ring on this one. Seed." He tossed it into the water.

"Okay," Kevin said. He glanced over at the boat that was in hailing distance of them. His girlfriend, Sheri, was on that boat with Frank Hussey, an older man, a Nantucket native who had scalloped all his life. Sheri was clearing off the board as Frank started to bring in a new tow. Although he was in his late fifties, Frank moved with the sinewy agility of a raccoon.

Looking over at Sheri, so placid and content, Kevin felt a sudden fit of pique. He didn't like being out on the water at all, having to be subservient to someone his own age. More than anything, he disliked not being good at what he was doing. He felt a certain disbelief that the world should put him in a situation where he wasn't good. But he wasn't about to give up. Even his decision to come to Nantucket hadn't been a retreat from his goal of a concert career as a violinist. He had come here to prepare for an important audition—to rediscover what was vital and true in his playing, away from the sterile atmosphere of graduate school. But he was finding—without fully realizing it—that it wasn't all that simple.

Russell finished the tow, turned off the outboard, and came forward to the culling board to help Kevin with the previous tow before bringing in the dredges. With the motor turned off, the sounds of the harbor stood out in sudden relief: water sloshing against the boat, the wind moaning around the stays, gulls crying. One gull let out a loud scream—E above middle C, with a quick glissando to F. Kevin looked all around but couldn't find the bird.

"Behind you," Russell said, with a small grin.

Kevin turned. The gull was on the front deck, glancing about with bright yellow eyes. It threw its head back, opened its mouth wide, and let fly another deep-throated cry. Kevin suddenly pictured the gull in a painting by Sheri, and then he pictured her painting, in a T-shirt and sweat pants. He glanced over toward the other boat again, and his pique gave way to the pride of possession.

Russell pried a scallop open and threw it to the gull. It pecked at the shell with sharp, quick motions, stopping every few seconds to look around for potential rivals, then swallowed the scallop in a clumsy gulp and flew off.

They culled for a few minutes and Kevin washed off a basketful and dumped the glistening scallops into a box.

"How many is that?" Russell asked.

"Let's see. Seven."

"Seven boxes," Russell said. "Not bad. We've turned the corner."

Kevin grunted in reply.

"Takes it out of you a little," Russell said. "All these heavy tows. I was up all night with the baby."

"What was wrong with him?"

"Teething. Chokes him right up. Doctor thinks he might have an asthmatic reaction."

"Can't you just leave him in his bed and let him cry himself to sleep?"

Russell looked directly at Kevin with a hint of reproach.

"I would never do that," he said. "If the baby's crying, he needs company. If you were crying, you'd need company."

Kevin didn't understand Russell's preoccupation with babies, but he usually felt good feelings coming from Russell when they discussed the subject. It relaxed Kevin, made him less anxious about mistakes. He threw a scallop down on the culling board to see if it was a dud. A dud would break apart when thrown down. But this one was clearly no dud; it hit the culling board so solidly that it bounced into the water.

"Oops," Russell said. "Careful, careful." His tone was more playful now, but retained a critical edge.

"Damn," Kevin said. "Culling by ordeal."

"By what?"

"By ordeal. Like in the Middle Ages. If it's a dud, it breaks and stays on the board. If it's good, it bounces off into the water."

"I just tap it," Russell said. "Tell by the sound."

"I guess I'm not that good yet."

"You will be. You'll get it."

"Yeah, maybe. Someday."

They culled off the rest of the board in silence. Kevin was thinking how someone should write a book about scalloping. There were endless title possibilities: *Everything You Always Wanted to Know About Scallops (But Were Afraid to Ask), Sex and the Single Scallop, The Scalloper Who Came In from the Cold.*

Russell started up the donkey engine—a small motor that turned the winch—and pulled in the front four dredges. They were starting to fill up the eighth box. Sheri and Frank had already gone in for the day. Russell knew, by rights, that he should finish before Frank, because his long warps fished the deep water in the Horseshed better than Frank's short warps. Russell took pride in the way he adapted his equipment to varying fishing conditions. That was one of the strange things about Frank: for all his experience and know-how, he wouldn't make certain adjustments, like lengthening his warps. Although Russell felt close to Frank and liked him, there were many things about the older man that he didn't understand and probably never would.

Kevin knocked another small adult off the board. Russell shook his head and worked on in silence.

CHAPTER 2

"**G**ood day?" Suzanne Hussey asked her husband when he came home after dropping his scallops off at the shanty.

"Not bad." Frank hung up his oilers on a peg in the pantry and sat down and pulled off his steel-reinforced boots. "They should open eight to eight and a half pounds a box, I guess."

"That's better than 'not bad,'" Suzanne said. "At five dollars a pound, that's downright good!"

A brief glimmer of amusement traveled over Frank's round face. He rarely allowed himself the luxury of yielding to laughter—not with his wife. Sometimes with his male cronies, over a beer or two. But not with Suzanne. Everything was quiet and understated with her, with tacit affection.

"Yeah, but I have to pay the culler, don't forget," he said.

"How is the new culler?" Suzanne had made no secret of her suspicions about his choice of Sheri for his mate, and Frank had met her half-humorous inquiries with a deliberately innocent response.

"Not bad," he said, aware of the resonance of the words.

12

"Oh?" Suzanne asked. "Would she also be an eight or an eight and a half? Or maybe a ten?"

Frank seemed to consider this question quite seriously. "Well, it depends on the standards you use," he said finally.

"Oh?"

"I mean, absolute or relative."

"And which do you use?"

Frank pondered this some more. "Relative, I suppose."

"And why's that?"

"Well, whatever she is, she's of no use to me unless I'm ready for it."

"I see. And are you ready for it?"

"Lord, no, Suzanne. You're all I can handle as it is."

Suzanne made a face, to show this was not acceptable. "What would you give her?"

"I think I'd have to call her a seven. Nice looks, nice personality, but too young for an old codger like me."

"Ugh!" Suzanne waved her arm at him, placed a cold beer in front of him, and started to leave the room. Frank grabbed her and pulled her onto his lap.

"Now this woman right here, I'd have to give her an eight and a half. This is a lot of woman for a guy like me to take advantage of."

"You think I'm fat."

"Well, it's like my Uncle Howie used to say about his wife: 'Miles and miles of it, and all of it mine.' "

"Thanks a lot," Suzanne said, smiling despite herself.

The door opened and their twenty-year-old daughter, Heather, came in.

"Jesus, Dad, don't you ever get enough?" she said, walking past them into the living room. She was short and slim and blond and moved with quick, decisive motions. Frank watched her with adoring eyes.

"Okay, let me up," Suzanne said. She stood and brushed back her straight, dark hair. At fifty, she was an attractive woman, with regular features and high, distinctive cheekbones. She wore her hair parted to the side, which somehow accentuated her bright blue eyes and wide, expressive mouth.

The words most frequently used to describe Suzanne were "a brick" and "a sweetheart." Any of her acquaintances with serious problems or big decisions to make came to her. It wasn't what she said so much as the feeling she gave. She instilled a sense wherever she went that things were right, that the world was good, that people were kind. Frank, watching her, sometimes just shook his head and wondered at his good fortune, that a clown like him had ended up with a woman like her. Now the thought skirted around the edge of his mind, not quite coming into focus, and made him wonder if he had forgotten to do something important. He was silent for a moment, trying without success to remember.

Frank and Suzanne lived on Mill Street, in a small, attractive house built right up next to the road, like most of the houses in town. Frank had inherited the house from his mother. In the early 1960s it would have sold for $20,000; in the mid-1980s it was worth half a million. Even with his healthy income from scalloping in the winter and quahogging in the summer, Frank could never afford to buy a house like it today. This didn't matter during his lifetime, since he already had the house, but it was getting to the point where it would be too expensive for his two kids to live on Nantucket. There was only the one house, and when he and Suzanne died it could hardly be split in two; if it were sold, half its value wouldn't buy much of a house for either kid, especially after inheritance taxes. There wasn't much future for a young man or woman on Nantucket anymore.

This $500,000 house had, upstairs, a bathroom and three bedrooms; downstairs, another bath, a kitchen, a living room-dining room, and a study; and, in the basement, a shop. Other houses on Nantucket with those features might sell for $200,000 less. What raised the value of Frank's house was that it was a "typical Nantucket house." It had been built in the early 1800s by a Quaker whaling captain and was a fine specimen of early Nantucket architecture, with its shingled sides, single central chimney, and plank frame windows. Inside, the historic features had been passed down unchanged from generation to generation: wide pine flooring, two working fireplaces, original paneling on the walls. It had a nice backyard even though the lot was relatively small. Around the perimeter, perpetually in need of repair, was an old picket fence. Just inside the fence, Suzanne had planted daffodils and tulips. Heather had always helped Suzanne, and when she was seventeen she began to market her services as a gardener and groundskeeper to the summer people. Now, three years later, she already had twenty-five clients.

Just up the hill from Frank and Suzanne was the Old Windmill, which still ground corn in the summer, when tourists would pay top dollar for it. It was the type of large, heavy-bladed windmill popularly associated with the Netherlands; the arms turned at a slow speed, even in the strongest wind. About half a mile outside town, there was a whole "windmill farm." These were the newer style of windmills, which resembled airplane propellers mounted on long poles. While the Old Windmill clanked and groaned under the weight of its burden, the new ones whizzed so fast that neighbors complained of interference in their television reception. And here on Nantucket, twenty-seven miles from the mainland, reception wasn't very good to begin with. Frank and Suzanne were among those lucky few in town who had cable, and their most frequent form of entertainment in the evenings was watching the Boston public television station, which always came in clear despite the distance and the windmills and the remoteness of their life in a small community far out at sea.

A few blocks away, on Pleasant Street, Sheri and Kevin were downstairs in the large house they had rented for the winter. During the summer this house went for $6,000 a month, but they had leased it for practically nothing over the winter, because the owners needed someone to take care of it.

While Sheri fixed a casserole for dinner, Kevin was practicing his violin. He was playing Bach's Chaconne, his favorite solo violin piece and one of the most technically challenging, especially the long arpeggiated section in the middle. Even for him, the section was not effortless or automatic.

In less than a month, Kevin had an audition in New York with a major talent agency, which had followed reviews of his concerts around Boston and in Connecticut. This might be his big break.

On the side table next to him there sat, unopened, a letter from his former counterpoint teacher and adviser at Harvard. Professor Blatt had written several times, asking when he was going to come back and get to work. Kevin felt a certain relief in leaving the letter unopened. Nothing appealed to him less than the thought that he would end up on the faculty of some music department somewhere. But that was where graduate school had been taking him—farther and farther from performance, deeper and deeper into the halls of academia. Was he really ready for that?

"Dinner's ready," Sheri said, standing in the doorway between the kitchen and the dining room.

"I'll be there in a minute," he replied, not pausing in his playing.

Sheri took the casserole out of the oven, poured a glass of wine for each of them, lit the candles, turned off the overhead light, and sat down at the table. She waited about ten minutes. Dinner was getting cold, but she tried not to get upset; it was good for Kevin to play a real piece. In recent weeks he had mostly been practicing studies, trying to solve little technical problems before the big audition. All that time he had been unusually self-contained and inaccessible.

Sheri had come to Nantucket that June, just after graduation, to work for the summer as a chambermaid and to visit her great-aunt, Maude Miller, who had lived on Nantucket for many years. Sheri fell in love with the island and decided to stay on that fall to paint and teach art part-time, and Kevin came to join her there after a summer in Aspen, Colorado, where he had been teaching assistant to a well-known Israeli virtuoso. Sheri had wondered if Kevin would really be happy on Nantucket, but despite her misgivings, she had been very glad he was coming. She found the house on Pleasant Street and moved there from her aunt's in late September. Kevin joined her a week later. She and Kevin had never really lived together before; the whole thing seemed like a wonderful adventure. But it was turning out to be more difficult than she had expected.

It could be trying to live with Kevin—petty things

irritated her, like worrying that dinner would be cold before he came. Sometimes it was hard when he focused on his own activity so much. But whenever Sheri had these thoughts, she made excuses for him. Kevin simply hadn't been himself recently. The scalloping was hard on him, much harder than it was on her. She didn't mind the break from her painting; it was a nice change. But Kevin was bothered by the hours away from his violin, the tedious, repetitive nature of the work, the cold and wet, the wind, the weather.

After a while she got up and gazed out the window at the thick, forbidding brick wall around Moor's End, the mansion across the street. When Kevin came in she quickly sat down at the table and dished out the casserole. It was cold, but he ate without seeming to taste anything.

Sheri looked at him and smiled. She knew she looked at her best in moonlight or candlelight, for it softened the straight, severe lines of her face. Sheri didn't think of herself as especially pretty. In fact, her face could be plain one moment and beautiful the next. Her long, straight dark hair and dark eyes gave her a certain air that made strangers stop and look at her, but she always felt they would be disappointed if they looked too long or too closely.

She reached over and patted Kevin on the hand. "Aunt Maude told me the other day that you seem to be a nice young man."

"How nice," he replied.

"You aren't pleased?"

"She isn't exactly my type."

"Oh, I know she's a little gruff sometimes, but she has a heart of gold."

Kevin didn't reply.

"What do you think of life on an island?" Sherry asked.

"Rather insular."

"Does that bother you?"

"Sometimes."

"Sometimes I have the feeling I don't have any clothes on."

"You don't, sometimes."

"Very funny. But I'm serious, Kevin. It's as though . . . everyone knows everything about me. It's scary."

Kevin shrugged.

Sheri took a breath and said, "I was thinking that we could have everyone over to dinner Friday night."

"Who?"

"Frank and his wife and Russell and his wife."

"Why?"

"It would be fun to get to know them all better."

"Sure, if you want." Kevin shrugged his shoulders and ate in silence.

Sheri could see something was bothering him. She lifted up her wineglass and said, "To the playing of my favorite violinist."

"Who, Chin? I noticed you listened to his Beethoven recording again last night." Chin was a young violinist who had attracted great attention in the past year as a possible successor to Stern and Perlman.

"You know I don't even like his playing that much. It's too strident, too lacking in subtlety," Sheri said carefully.

Kevin agreed quickly.

"He's the equivalent of a banger on the piano."

"I think you play as well as him."

"Thanks a lot."

"What?"

"You tell me you don't like his playing, and then you say I play as well as him."

"I only meant—"

"I should hope I play better."

"Well, you do. I just meant that with everyone getting so excited about him . . ."

Kevin pushed himself away from the table and stood up with a jerky motion intended to indicate, once and for all, his displeasure.

"Thanks for dinner," he told her.

He walked out into the living room and started to practice chromatic scales in octaves—the one exercise that Sheri could not bear to listen to. She pushed her plate away and rested her head in her hands. She had to remember he wasn't normally like this; something was eating at him.

After a few minutes, her thoughts wandered to more pleasant subjects. She thought of the dinner she would have Friday. She looked up Frank's and Russell's phone numbers. But before she called, she found herself thinking about Frank, about the unspoken kindness he showed her.

Sheri had found her mate position a few weeks before Kevin got his. In mid-October, she and Kevin had realized they were rapidly running out of money. When Heather—one of Sheri's art students—happened to mention that her father needed a culler, Sheri called Frank up that night and got the job on Heather's recommendation.

Besides the $60 a day she would earn, scalloping appealed to Sheri for aesthetic reasons—what better way for an artist to get to know the water? But so far, Sheri had hardly noticed the water; her head was always bent over the culling board. It was something of a shock, but it was fun, too, and a challenge. She had learned quickly how to spot the adult scallops, and she and Frank often finished two hours earlier than Kevin and Russell. She didn't think she had anything to do with this; it must be because Frank was an older, more experienced captain than Russell. She wouldn't believe that she could be better than Kevin at anything. When they were both at Harvard, it was always he who had won the awards and received the attention, for his violin, his compositions. While she enjoyed painting, no one else had seemed particularly impressed by what she did.

The one thing she couldn't help noticing on the boat was how picturesque Frank was, with his round weathered face, his unusual eyes (one of them was almost gray, the other a golden brown), and his thick mat of blond hair, which had not a strand of gray—only a few white hairs at the temples. There was something about him that comforted her. She felt a daughterly affection for him already. He didn't speak much, but when he did he was invariably polite. He seemed to live by a code she was only dimly beginning to understand. He never complained, even though he was obviously tired by the end of the day. And he never swore, although she had heard that the language of fishermen was atrocious. He had one odd mannerism that she found endearing: just before he did anything new, like setting a new tow or opening up his thermos and pouring out some coffee, he said "Umm-huh," as though in agreement to something she had said. But of course, she had said nothing; there had been no conversation at all. This mannerism established a bond between them, somehow included her in his private thoughts, as though she were his daughter and not some virtual stranger who just happened to be on his boat six days a week.

Kevin had gone on to arpeggio exercises. Sheri sighed, stood up, and cleared off the table. Carefully, she put his glass of wine aside for later; they would have a glass each before they went to bed. Maybe Kevin would be feeling better by then.

Half an hour later, Kevin came into the room. "You're nice to put up with a maniac like me."

She took his glasses off—which always gave his eyes a gentle, unfocused expression that she liked—and said, "I just wish you wouldn't push yourself so hard."

"It's the only way to be really good," he replied.

He came over and hugged her. Looking over his shoulder, she gave a scream.

"What's wrong?"

"There's a fish in that bucket!"

Kevin turned and looked, taking his glasses from her.

"Oh, I forgot," he said. "Russell gave me a flounder to take home for dinner."

Sheri walked closer to the dead fish. "Get it out of here!" she exclaimed. "It's gross."

"It's just a dead fish," he said.

"Get it out!"

"Okay, okay."

Kevin carried the fish outside. When he came back in, Sheri was already in the bathroom, brushing her teeth. She was wearing her bedclothes: sweat pants and a sweatshirt, on the front of which was a picture of a scallop and the legend, *Scalloping is dredgery.* Kevin came up to her and ran his hands along her back.

"Why did that fish bother you so much?"

"I don't know." She took him by the hand and led him into the bedroom.

*   *   *

22

Russell was still at the shanty, hanging around, talking to the openers. He liked the shanty, liked the camaraderie there, the relaxed but busy mood as the openers cut away at the scallops. Although to the casual observer the shanty might seem messy and disorganized, with broken shells and scallop guts littering the cement floor, Russell saw only the next boxes of unopened scallops and the orderly activity at the benches. When the scallops were small and hard to open, he usually opened a box or two himself, to help out. When they were large, he kept his hands off. Openers liked to keep the large scallops to themselves, because they could make almost twice as much per hour from large scallops as from small ones.

One of Russell's openers was Frank's son, Mike. He was new, just a kid, and occasionally Russell took the knife from him and demonstrated something to help him out. A scallop is opened with a special knife, a short blunt blade of rounded metal with a wooden or fiberglass handle. The knife is inserted into the side with a motion that cuts the muscle at the top, where it joins the shell. The muscle has to be cut right at the top, or some of the eye is wasted. This motion also pushes the top shell up and away. Then the knife is laid down at the back, square to the shell, and pulled forward with a rolling motion that lifts the guts over and off the eye. Finally, the eye is scraped off the bottom shell and tossed into a plastic bucket.

A highly skilled opener works so fast that an eye is practically always up in the air, on the way from shell to bucket.

Russell noticed that Mike was making two mistakes. He was holding the scallop over the bucket as he opened, allowing pieces of gut and dirt to fall in with the eyes. And he was turning the knife blade under as he scraped the knife forward, thus nicking the eye. The result was that he was slow and wasteful—opening only about six pounds an hour of really nice stuff that someone else could do twice as quickly.

All his life, Mike had avoided scalloping, despite pressure from his father. (Frank had started scalloping on Saturdays at age seven.) As Frank's friend, Russell felt a responsibility to train Mike right; he wanted Mike to do well. Mike was clearly trying hard, with a dogged if unfocused determination to prove himself.

So whenever Russell tried to correct Mike's bad habits, he spoke in jovial tones, though he was tired and hungry and exasperated from the long day on the water.

Other scallopers, coming in to check on their openers, greeted Russell loudly and warmly. He was popular among them, known for his hard work, his strength, his good sense. He had something about him, a kind of charisma. He set the tone of conversations; people respected him.

"Jeez." Roger, one of the other scallopers, came over to take a look at the catch. "Beautiful stuff. Were you working the jetty?"

"Naw, Horseshed," Russell said, in a tone that showed it wasn't really as good as it looked. The last thing he wanted was for the other guys to realize how well he was doing at Horseshed. Then the whole fleet would be over there, and they would work the area out in a few days. As it was, Russell hoped to get at least a couple of weeks of good fishing there.

"Nice stuff," Roger said, examining the eyes in the bucket. "Huge eyes. Look at 'em! Big as quarters!"

"It was a lot of work," Russell said, with a shrug. "I didn't get in till three, three thirty." He knew he would have been in by noon with a good culler, but he didn't say that.

"Worth it, I'd say," Roger persisted. He stared at Russell; there was a slightly unbalanced look in his eye. "Don't tell me it wasn't worth it, Russell." He nodded his bearded face at Russell, almost menacingly.

"Naw. That stuff of yours, that's opening real nice," Russell said, pointing toward Roger's bench.

"Seven pounds a box." Now it was Roger's turn to shrug.

"That's not bad."

"Bad compared to what you'll get out of this."

"I might get seven, seven and a half. Lot of duds there."

As if to underscore this point, Mike stuck his knife into a scallop, and two empty shells fell away into the plastic trash can protruding halfway out from under the bench.

"How's your culler doing?" Roger asked.

"I think he'll work out okay, once he gets a little more experience," Russell said.

"Frank's got a nice-looking culler this year."

"Yeah. My guy's girlfriend," Russell said. "Nice girl. Well, see you later, Rog." He went off to talk to the owner of the shanty about payment. The shanty bought the scallops at wholesale, deducting a $50-a-week fee for use of the benches, and Russell was waiting for his check from the previous week—which should be almost $2,500.

Roger remained behind, watching Mike open.

"You're cutting his fish," he told Mike.

Mike made an angry, impatient gesture but didn't reply.

"You're cutting his fish," Roger repeated.

"So what?" Mike said, with a shrug.

"You're losing money for him. He should be getting more weight than that. Look, you're not scraping the whole eye out. Look at that!" Roger picked a shell out of the trash can and waved it in front of Mike. A small piece of scallop eye clung to the inside.

"What of it?" Mike asked belligerently.

"You should be more careful."

Mike didn't reply.

"How come you started opening this year, anyway? You never did before," Roger asked.

"I wanted to."

"I know why. You're trying to get money for dope. You don't care what kind of a job you do, you just want your dope."

"What's it to you?"

"Russell's my friend, that's what."

"Bug off!"

Roger frowned. "The last guy who talked to me like that ended up in the hospital."

Mike glared at Roger. His pupils were so dilated that only a thin strip of iris showed. "You trying to scare me?"

Roger wagged a finger at him. "You better watch yourself," he said.

Mike swerved and shook his scallop knife under Roger's face. "You shut up or I'll cut your face," he warned.

Roger slapped the knife to the side and took a step back. "Watch it, punk!" he shouted. Everyone in the shanty turned to look. "Watch it!"

"Take it easy, Mike!" a few of the other openers yelled. But Mike raised his knife again and shouted, "You watch it! All of you!"

Russell walked in then, saw the commotion, and said, "Hey, Mike, what the hell's going on here?"

"Nothing," Mike said. He respected Russell's superior size and status.

26

"I'm paying you to open, not get in fights, right?"

"Yeah, right," Mike said, turning back to the bench.

"I want no more of that, understand?" Russell said.

Mike just shook his head and was quiet. The other openers turned back to their work.

The owner of the shanty, a large man with a bushy moustache, came into the room, carrying a bucketful of shucked sea scallops. Although sea scallops are the same shape as bay scallops, the difference between the two is striking: sea scallops are pure white, while bay scallops are pale orange; and sea scallops are almost twice as large as bay scallops. The owner dumped the bucketful of sea scallops onto a bench and separated out the smaller ones. Russell came over beside him and made a clucking sound with his tongue.

"I know what you're doing," he said.

The owner smiled.

"Naughty, naughty," Russell went on. "Buying sea scallops that are too small to sell and then passing them off as bay scallops."

"They taste the same."

"No, they don't. Sea scallops are like mud compared to bay scallops. And why sea scallops bring a higher price than bay scallops, I'll never understand."

"It's the markets, Russell. You can't help the markets."

"Five dollars a pound for our beautiful bay scallops. That's too low, when sea scallops go for six. And those guys don't have to work nearly as hard for them as we do."

"You're doing okay, from what I can tell."

Russell shook his head and walked away.

A few minutes later, Russell went outside, past the stench of the scallop guts waiting to be hauled away, and got into his old Toyota pickup. He drove home, to the cottage he and his wife rented. In his free time away from scalloping (which wasn't much), Russell was building their own house, on a piece of property he and Mary had bought a few years ago, before land prices were quite so inflated. He wondered about going over there tonight, after dinner, and putting up some wallboard but decided against it. He was too tired today.

When he opened the front door, Sam, his year-old son, let out a scream. Sam started to walk over to him but couldn't go fast enough, so he got down and crawled. Russell got down too and crawled toward Sam. They met halfway across the living room and stopped, eyeing each other for a moment. Then Russell picked Sam up, tossed him into the air, and caught him. Sam let himself go limp in his daddy's arms, with a burst of laughter. Mary, peeking around the door from the kitchen, smiled and went back to her cooking. She was already big again, expecting another child.

After dinner, Mary went to her weekly chorus rehearsal. It was Russell's night to babysit. Normally, he loved to be with Sam, but something was happening to him, now that scalloping season had started. He had to be busy every moment, or he didn't know what to do with himself.

He put the car bed in the Toyota and drove off to the shanty. He knew the motion of the truck would put Sam to sleep earlier than his normal bedtime, which meant Sam would wake up in the middle of the night, to everyone's disadvantage. But he couldn't help himself. He left Sam sleeping while he went into the shanty and checked on the openers. Everything was fine; he wasn't needed, but he hung around for half an hour.

On the way home he stopped off at the Chicken Box, crowded up to the bar, and exchanged pleasantries with his friends. He wasn't there to drink—he only had a soda—but he couldn't stay away from the other fish-ermen, from the whole scalloping scene. He left just in time to get back home before Mary.

When she came in, Sam was asleep in bed, and Russell told her they had spent a nice evening together. Seeing the restless expression in his eyes, Mary won-dered, but she didn't say anything.

CHAPTER 3

The next morning promptly at six Russell pulled up in front of Kevin's house. There was a faint tinge of pink in the east; a pale light lay over the gray shingled houses and the yards and the streets. Kevin emerged from the house carrying his oilers and a paper bag with a sandwich and a small can of V-8 juice. Sheri came out behind him, already in her oilers. As Kevin put his things in the back of the truck she walked by, on the way to Frank's house.

"Good morning," Russell said to her in the suave voice he reserved for attractive members of the opposite sex. (He thought Sheri had one of the sexiest pairs of lips he had ever seen.) He spoke through the window, which he always left down, even in the coldest weather; the crank was broken, and he had never bothered to fix it. "Offer you a ride?"

"No, thanks," she replied, with the pleasant smile that seemed hearty and gutsy for such a slight girl. "I like the walk." Her dark brown hair showed at the edges of her oiler hood.

"Maybe she's ashamed to be seen in my truck," Russell confided to Kevin, with a wink, as Kevin sat down beside him.

Kevin made a slight motion of his mouth, to show he wasn't especially interested in the whole issue.

This lack of response goaded Russell into a further discussion of the subject of his truck. As he let out the clutch and drove off toward the dock, he said, "You know, when my three-year-old nephew heard I'd bought a Toyota, he was real excited. The next time he came to visit, I showed him the truck. I expected, you know, a good response from him. But naw, nothing. Was he disappointed! For the longest time I couldn't figure out why. He kept searching through the truck, saying, 'I can't find it, I can't find it.' Turned out he thought I had a toy Yoda—you know, the Star Wars guy."

Russell turned to Kevin, expecting this to get at least a little rise from him, but Kevin continued to look impassively at the road in front of them.

"What's the matter, you have a bad night or something?"

"No, I'm fine."

"We're gonna try a new area today—the jetty. It's cleaner out there, should be faster culling. Thought you might appreciate that."

"All the same to me either way."

Russell almost said, Yeah, well, it's not the same to me. You're too goddam slow, you know. But he restrained himself.

Twin jetties extend out into Nantucket Sound far beyond the mouth of the harbor. The tide races through the opening between the jetties, which is several yards wide. Slack tide—when the tide is not moving at all, at either its highest or lowest point—often lasts for an hour or more at other places in the harbor, but at the jetties it lasts no more than a few minutes. The tide is always on the move. This strong tide not only keeps the bottom unusually clean, it also produces scallops that are among the largest and healthiest bay scallops in the world—opening ten or more pounds a box. The tide brings such a wealth of nutrients that even the seed scallops there are larger than the adult scallops in the rest of the harbor.

Scalloping at the jetties is generally an all-day affair. Although the catch is quite clean, there are not a lot of scallops there, and a high percentage is seed. Long tows are needed to fill the dredges.

Russell's decision to go there, which had come to him in the middle of the night when he got up with Sam, was not merely intended to make the culling easier for Kevin. He was also worried that word was getting around about Horseshed. He figured if he was seen there today, a whole fleet would join him. But if he went to the jetty for a few days, there was a chance he might be able to go back to Horseshed and have it all to himself again. That was the thing about scallops: unlike fish, the tide doesn't ever bring in any more. Every one of them has to grow there, for a period of more than a year, before it can be caught and sold. Once they're gone, they're gone.

As Russell turned down Main Street, the old truck shook and jostled over cobblestones that dated back to the late eighteenth century. He made a few more turns, skirted the docks down at Straight Wharf, went past the old shanties that had been converted into summer art galleries, and drove on until he came to the dock at Children's Beach. He backed the truck up to the dock and left Kevin to unload the boxes and the extra gas can while he rowed his dinghy out to the mooring. Russell had an old, wide, heavy, wooden fishing boat, which had earned the nickname "PT boat." But although it was big and clumsy to look at, it had been a good boat. Russell had bought it four years earlier for just $1,400. Fiberglassing the bottom had cost him an additional $2,000, and he spent a couple of hundred dollars a year on paint. But in just four years with the boat, he had cleared over $125,000 from scalloping in the winter and quahogging in the summer.

At times he felt twinges of resentment toward the boat. He felt he deserved better, felt he deserved the more prestigious Sea Ox that fishermen like Frank owned. The Sea Ox was all fiberglass, required almost no upkeep, and was faster. Still, Russell was proud of his old tank. It reminded him of where he had come from. It wasn't so long ago that he bought the boat and it had seemed the most beautiful thing in the world. He remembered that stage of his life with pride. He had worked hard to escape it, worked hard to get to the point where he could own his own land and house. Soon, that dream would become reality.

Bands of yellow lit the eastern sky as Russell brought his boat up to the dock. Other scallopers were gathering there now, pausing a minute or two to chat.

"Going back to Horseshed?" someone asked Russell.

"Naw. Too messy there. I'm going hunting today," he replied with a smile.

Kevin threw the plastic mesh scallop boxes into the boat. He handed the extra gas tank to Russell and hopped into the bow.

Russell's engine was only a 50-horsepower—barely strong enough to bring the boat to a plane. It was four years old, and Russell was worried about it; if it died at a crucial point in a tow, the lines could become hopelessly tangled. But it sounded good this morning as they steered along the channel, past the Horseshed. Frank and Sheri waved as they went by. Sheri was already culling off the first tow.

Russell steered out to the west jetty and set his tow, throwing in the dredges first on the port side, then the starboard. He watched the warps carefully as they uncoiled. With the boat moving ahead at five knots and all eight lines uncoiling at the same time, tangles were inevitable. There were stories of fishermen who were caught in the warps and pulled overboard and drowned, but it always seemed to happen on the Cape or in the Vineyard—never on Nantucket.

The tow was a long one, almost twenty minutes. Kevin stood silently by the culling board. The motor hummed along. It sounded to Kevin like someone chanting a mantra. He thought of a good article for *National Lampoon*—"The Zen of Scalloping" or some such thing, how all is one in the hum of existence. What would a scallop say if it reached nirvana, "Yummy bottom"?

He smiled slightly, and Russell said, "What's so funny?"

"Nothing," Kevin said. Russell jerked his head to the side and raised his eyebrows.

Every few minutes, Russell grabbed one of the warps and pulled at it, to gauge how full the dredges were and what they were picking up. If they bounced along the bottom, they were probably full of scallops. If they slid with a kind of rolling motion, they were grassed up. These dredges were bouncing along nicely. It felt promising.

He cut the motor and started up the donkey with the pull cord. The donkey was mounted under the culling board and made the whole board shake. Russell pulled in the front dredge on the port side until he had enough slack to loop it up into the block on the frame overhead. He wound the warp around the winch and allowed the rotation of the winch to bring the dredge in. Beads of water flew off the warp in the wind. Stray pieces of eelgrass tumbled onto the board. The dredge took shape in the water a few feet away from the boat. It pulled free of the water and swung up onto the board. Russell turned it around and dumped it, first the right side, then the left.

"Looks pretty full," Kevin remarked, over the roar of the donkey.

"Yeah, not bad," Russell said. He picked up a scallop. "But be careful. This big guy is seed. See? No growth ring."

"Okay, I'll look out for that."

"Remember, if we bring in anything more than five-percent seed, we can be docked for a couple days, even longer." He grinned. "I remember one time, three–four years ago, when Frank got a *week* for too much seed. He had spread a few adults on top, but underneath it was all seed. The warden told Frank to dump out a box so he could look through it, and Frank dumped 'em out right on the street and just walked away. He knew he'd been caught."

Russell brought in three more dredges and turned off the donkey. Kevin had only put about ten scallops into the basket. He was holding up a large one now, a few inches away from his eyes.

"What's the matter?" Russell asked.

"I can't find the growth ring on some of these," Kevin said.

"If you can't find one, it's probably a seed," Russell said. He picked up a series of scallops and said, in quick succession, "Seed, seed, adult, seed, seed, adult, adult, seed, seed, seed."

Kevin was holding up another scallop, scrutinizing it.

"Come on, Kevin, let's go. It's either an adult or it isn't."

Something snapped in Kevin then. He began to throw in every scallop that was of a decent size. Russell, glad to see Kevin moving faster, didn't check his work. He turned and brought in the rest of the dredges.

They finished by noon and headed back toward the dock.

"Not bad," Russell said. "You're getting the hang of it."

"Yeah, I guess so," Kevin said.

Russell bent down and examined one of the boxes. He picked off a few scallops and threw them into the water.

"Couple of seed on top," he said. He had a lingering doubt in the back of his mind, but he didn't think about it any more.

Frank and Sheri were just finishing their seventh box. Frank didn't know if his wife had implanted the thought in his mind, but he was beginning to find something awfully attractive about this girl. She was so free of airs, so natural, so cheerful. And she was nice-looking, with her dark hair and eyes. In the middle of the dirtiest work out on the boat, she always looked clean and fresh, pure. She was at that age when you can tell a woman wants to be married, wants to settle down with a husband and raise a family. He knew she had a boyfriend, but he suspected it was only a temporary arrangement. She wasn't totally happy about it, that was his impression.

As she bent over to pour a basket into the seventh

box, Frank observed her slender figure, easy to notice despite her oilers. She brought out some feeling in him that had long been dormant—the feeling that a pretty girl was in need of a champion. It was more than sexual. It was an appeal to the side of him that wanted to be a hero, a protector.

Russell pulled up alongside. "Careful, Frank, I got her boyfriend here," Russell said. "The only bottom you should be interested in is the bottom of the harbor."

"Just making sure she was crowning up the boxes good, Russell," Frank replied. "Well, you get 'em today?"

"Yeah, we got 'em pretty quick," Russell said. "Nice clean stuff out there."

"I'm surprised you left here, with the weight we're getting."

"It's even better out at the jetty."

"Yeah, but there's an awful lot of seed."

"It wasn't too bad, was it, Kevin?" Russell asked.

"Hi, Kevin," Sheri said, standing up and blushing.

"Not too bad," Kevin replied. His brown eyes glanced through his wire-rim glasses with quick, penetrating looks that left a sense of distaste behind them.

Russell lifted one of the boxes onto the culling board and brought the boat over next to Frank. Frank reached out and pawed through the top of the box.

"I hate to say this, Russell, but you got fifty percent seed in there."

"What? No," Russell said.

"Take a look for yourself."

Russell dumped out the box on the culling board and went through it.

"Jesus Christ, Kevin," he said. "We brought in practically all seed."

"We did?" Kevin asked, in a dull, unconcerned tone.

"It looks awfully big for seed," Sheri said in his defense.

"It's seed, though," Frank said. "You can see by the flatness of the shell. Well, what will it be, Russ? Gonna try to sneak it by the warden?" Taking advantage of the pause in the rhythm of the day, Frank lit up a cigarette. For years he had been trying to stop smoking, with no success.

"You kidding? You think I want to lose a week in November? No way. We're dumping this overboard and starting over," Russell said.

"Try this tow. Line up with the town clock and the old foundation of the shed. I'm getting close to two boxes a tow at slack," Frank told him.

"Yeah, thanks," Russell said. He shoved the motor into gear and went off quickly, angrily, to the start of the tow. Sheri waved to Kevin with an apologetic expression on her face, as if she somehow were responsible for the problem. Half an hour later, she and Frank went in for the day.

Russell set the dredges in silence and turned back toward Kevin.

"Go ahead, dump it all over," he said.

"All of it?" Kevin asked. "Can't we even save the good stuff?"

"How can we save it, when you don't know what it looks like?"

Kevin did as he was told, bristling. But he didn't protest. He knew he deserved whatever anger Russell felt toward him. But that made him resent Russell all the more.

They worked on, in silence.

At one thirty a distant roar announced that the Concorde was overhead; it flew over Nantucket twice a day on its way to Europe. Russell stopped to look for it, a tiny, distinct flame of silver in the vast blue sky, and watched until it passed directly overhead and blurred to chalky white. Then he went back to work. Seconds later a muffled boom echoed across the water.

They had three boxes, mainly through Russell's efforts: he was hauling in the dredges and culling off the board with herculean speed and strength. Across the board from him, Kevin worked as hard as he could, out of some dogged need to show that he could, after all, do the work. But despite their efforts, they had only eight boxes by four, and according to law they could work no later than four thirty. Fortunately, it was slack tide again, and the last tow just filled up the tenth box.

"We're gonna be too late for one of my openers," Russell said as they came up to the dock. The gray Nantucket dusk, the color of weathered shingles, was melting away the buildings. "You're gonna have to open two boxes for me."

"I don't know how," Kevin said.

"You're gonna have to learn."

Kevin didn't argue. He could have gone either way at that point, either walked away or stuck it out. He didn't know why, unless it was that he had never failed at anything before, but he decided to stick it out. He didn't even consider that Russell might fire him. He had never been fired in his life, and it was inconceivable that someone his own age would do it.

"I'll drop you off at home. Grab a bite to eat, and in a half hour I'll be back," Russell said. He let Kevin out and drove away, honking and waving at a friend he spotted, as if it had been the easiest, best day of his life.

"You get 'em all?" Sheri asked with a smile when Kevin came inside. This was the traditional greeting of one returning scalloper to another, and it was one of their private jokes to talk to each other that way.

"Yeah. We got 'em," Kevin said.

"I called Suzanne and Mary. Dinner is all set for tomorrow."

Kevin didn't respond. Sheri had never seen him look so tired and pathetic. His glasses were smeared, his face was dirty, his oilers were covered with salt and seaweed.

Sheri went over and hugged him. "My poor fisherman. You've had a long day."

"It's not over yet."

"Why not?" she asked, taking off his glasses and blowing on his eyes.

Kevin grabbed his glasses out of her hand. "I got to open a couple of boxes tonight."

"Why?"

"We came in too late for one of the openers."

"But your hands!" Sheri said. "You could hurt your hands!"

Kevin just shrugged.

"Kevin, I can't let you go there and open scallops. Even if you don't cut yourself, the scallop juice will ruin your hands. I've heard about what it does. It makes them all rough and dry."

"I'll wear gloves."

"I don't understand how you could put yourself through something like this."

"I'm not putting myself through anything. I'm doing what I want to do."

"Let me open them, Kevin. Please."

"No, thanks," he said. He walked into the bathroom and slammed the door. Sheri put some food on the table for him. Then she slipped outside and walked at a fast clip toward the shanty. She had a distinctive way of walking: it was as though her shoulders pulled her forward. Kevin sometimes told her that the dutiful, driven part of her resided in her shoulders and controlled her motions.

Eagerly, Sheri breathed in the moist air, which smelled of leaves and salt water. A pale yellow light lay over the town, silent and peaceful. Wild roses still bloomed, climbing up fences and trellises. In the dim light they had little color, but their texture and depth were enhanced. The rose hips were large and ripe, ready to burst with seed. In the distance, Sheri could just make out the roof of Frank and Suzanne's house. She looked toward it in the mild evening light and felt, suddenly, very free and happy.

She cut down Fair Street to Main, past the majestic Pacific National Bank building (what was a Pacific Bank doing in the middle of the Atlantic Ocean? she wondered), and continued down the middle of Main. On either side of the wide cobblestoned street, granite curbstones rose to brick sidewalks dotted with street-lamps and curving, gracious benches. The buildings with their brick or clapboard fronts—two pharmacies, a bookstore, two insurance agencies, various shops and realtors—rose against the dusk in full relief, freed of the summer crowds. The street itself was nearly empty of automobiles, except for a few pickup trucks, some older American sedans, and a new Volvo station wagon. The cobblestones reminded Sheri of fossilized dinosaur eggs, they seemed so large and ancient, and she liked the rolling, irregular motion they gave to her walk. She walked on, past a series of gray shingled buildings. The shanty was behind a fish market not far from the harbor. As she came closer an odor grew stronger with each step: the stench of scallop guts.

CHAPTER 4

Early that afternoon, Mary O'Grady had gone to visit Suzanne. Like many of the young married women on Nantucket, she found a special friend in Frank's wife: Suzanne was so comforting and cheering and full of good advice about any number of problems, from diaper rash to a husband who was too often away. Mary was sometimes lonely during the day when Russell went out fishing. It wasn't that she didn't have enough to do. She was always behind on the lightship baskets she made and sold through local gift and craft stores. Sam, of course, demanded a lot of attention and care, which she gave freely and without resentment. And just keeping up with the cleaning and cooking and shopping was quite a chore when you had a little one and were pregnant too. But still, Mary had days when she felt lonely—maybe overwhelmed was a better word—and at times like that she had a yearning to see Suzanne.

Preparing for the visit, Mary dressed Sam in his sailor suit; she always liked Suzanne to see him at his best.

"Come on, Sam," she said. "Let's go see Suzanne."

"Zan!" Sam said. He already knew her by name—

the only person he knew besides Mommy, Daddy, and Harry the cat.

When they arrived Suzanne was working at her loom. Mary knocked on the door and pushed it open shyly.

"I hope I'm not interrupting," she said.

"Don't be silly!" Suzanne told her. "Hello, Sambo." She came over and gave Sam a kiss on the cheek. Mary looked around uncertainly, and Suzanne said, "Sit down, girl, sit down! You're just in time to give me your opinion of this mess I've gotten myself into." She went on to demonstrate a problem with the blanket she was weaving. She described it in such a way that there was clearly only one solution, but when Mary suggested it, Suzanne made Mary feel as though she never would have thought of it herself.

Suzanne had the rare gift of never seeming too busy to see other people. No matter what she was doing when visitors arrived, she simply made room in the middle of her activity, like parting water. More often than not she was weaving on the large loom that Frank had made for her. She made beautiful blankets and shawls of warm browns and grays—those were Suzanne's colors, the colors of the island in winter. Her blankets were very popular and always sold out at Nantucket Looms.

After she found Sam some toys and got him settled on the floor, Suzanne went back to the loom and resumed her work. Mary sat beside Sam, playing with him and talking to Suzanne.

"I'm worried about Russell," Mary told her.

"Why?" Suzanne asked.

"He's pushing himself too hard. He's getting exhausted. He just isn't himself. He acts like he used to when he was drinking."

Suzanne looked over at Mary, and her eyes made contact in a way that Mary felt with no other person on earth but Sam.

"Building a house is the biggest strain on a family there is," Suzanne said. "I've seen it time and again. The weakest link in the family will break. A daughter needs to go off-island to school. A wife has to go stay with her mother for a few months. A husband starts drinking."

"But if he just took it easy . . ."

"Mary, would you love Russell if he was the type who took it easy?"

This made Mary stop and think. "No," she said.

"Fix him a big dinner. Get him to relax. Get Sam to bed early, so you have some time alone. You know how to make him happy and forget about everything else."

"I guess I get upset too."

"You don't need to. You have a wonderful child, a wonderful husband, and soon you'll have a wonderful house. How many people can say that?"

Mary came over and gave Suzanne a hug. Suzanne returned the hug only briefly: Mary had the passing sense that Suzanne might be more elusive than she let on.

It also seemed to Mary that Suzanne was glancing at the clock more frequently than usual, as though wondering what might be keeping Frank. She seemed flustered, maybe even a little lonely herself. Once or twice Mary said she should be leaving, but Suzanne prevailed upon her to stay longer.

Mary and Sam were still there when Frank came home from scalloping about two.

"Hi, honey," Suzanne said, rising and going to the stove. "I've got lunch waiting for you." Mary watched Suzanne carefully, observing the effortless way she moved from working at the loom to serving lunch.

"Lunch? How about my beer?" Frank asked, with a wink toward Mary. He picked up Sam and swung him over his shoulder. Sam chortled.

"Here it is," Suzanne said, taking Sam from him and handing him a beer. "Have a good day today?"

"Not bad," Frank said, sitting down at the table.

"How's your culler doing?"

Frank was looking the newspaper over and didn't answer.

"Honey?" Suzanne asked.

"What? Fabulous, fabulous," he said, with exaggerated enthusiasm to show that he was kidding. But Mary detected something out of place in the humor, and she glanced toward Suzanne to see if she noticed it too. Suzanne showed no response. She was already threading a new warp onto the loom, with Sam standing at her side.

"I forget to tell you. She called last night. We're all invited to dinner tomorrow night. Russell and Mary too."

"That's nice," Frank said, from behind his newspaper.

"Do you know if Russell is in yet?" Mary asked.

"Russell?" Frank pushed his newspaper away with a hint of annoyance at all these questions. But he immediately regained his habitual courtesy. "Oh, yeah, poor Russell. His culler threw pure seed into his boxes today. They had to dump it all out and start over. They'll be out all day."

"Isn't that Sheri's boyfriend?" Suzanne asked.

"I think I heard something about that," Frank said. He sipped at the bottle of beer reflectively.

"Don't you remember? Heather told us."

"I guess I forgot," he said. He seemed vaguely annoyed.

"I don't think Russell is too happy with him," Mary said. "He won't say anything, though."

"You mark my words, he'll never admit it to anyone, not even you. He'll never admit he hired the wrong man, unless the culler is absolutely awful!" Frank said suddenly, looking up angrily.

"Why ever not?" Suzanne asked. She began working the pedals of the loom with her feet.

"Because that's the way of young guys," Frank said. "A young guy can never admit it when he makes a mistake. You got to be old like me, get knocked around awhile, before you learn how to do that."

"Oh, you're not that old," Suzanne told him. "You don't even have any gray hairs."

"I'm getting there," Frank said, burping and shaking his head. "Yep, I'm getting there."

It irked Mary that he was implicitly criticizing Russell. Frank, after all, was the reason that Russell first came to Nantucket: in New Bedford several years before, Russell had joined the crew of Frank's offshore fishing vessel, which put in at Nantucket. Russell had quickly worked his way up to be Frank's second mate and still maintained a strong affection for the older man, regarding him almost like a father. It seemed to Mary that Frank ignored those ties when he talked that way about Russell.

"Russell may surprise you, Frank," she said. "Once he reaches his threshold on something, he forgets about pride. If he gets too upset with his culler, he'll find somebody else, you watch."

"We'll see about that," Frank said. "There's certain things young guys just don't know about." He lit a cigarette.

"Honey, I thought you were stopping," Suzanne said.

46

"Jesus Christ, it's getting to the point where I can only smoke out on my boat!" Frank exclaimed, taking up the paper again. "At least my culler doesn't tell me what to do."

Sam pushed himself up against the table and walked over to Mary. He was whimpering, as he always did when he sensed unhappiness in the air.

Mary took Sam home a little while later, put him down for a nap, and had a big, hot meal prepared for Russell when he came in.

"I better just grab a snack," he said. "One of the openers is sick. I gotta open a few boxes. Then I'll come back and be able to really relax."

"Oh, just eat a little," Mary said. She had vowed not to be upset when he came home—to make him feel loved and help him relax—but already she was losing it. She hated it, this tug on their time together during scalloping season. If the men had their way, all family life would cease from November through February. It wasn't as if she didn't know what it was like out there; she had been Russell's culler for a little while before Sam was born. But even then she had known it wasn't always necessary to wear yourself out and stay out all day. The men feared coming in short more than being cold or exhausted.

"I can't, honey," Russell said. "I can't help it if an opener is sick." It really seemed to Russell that one of the openers *was* sick; he didn't want to mention his troubles with Kevin.

"Your culler slowed you up today, didn't he?" Mary said.

Russell stared at her. "How did you know?"

"I was over at Suzanne's when Frank came home."

"He's gonna be okay," Russell said. "I'd have to open tonight anyway."

Mary felt him slipping away, slipping off into the world of scalloping.

"Russell, you've got to watch it. You're pushing yourself too hard. Something's going to give way. You can't scallop ten hours a day and build a house too, all by yourself."

"Well, who's going to help me?" he asked. "Answer me that." He gave her a hard, unfeeling look.

"All right, go on back then," Mary said, tears welling up in her eyes. She had the odd thought that these were really Suzanne's tears, that some kind of bad feeling in the air at Suzanne's had followed her home.

"Honey," Russell said, "we're building a house. I gotta do what I gotta do."

"I said go ahead," she repeated. She was crying, but at the same time she felt she was being stupid and childish. Sam began to cry from his room.

"Jesus, I work hard all day and look what I get for it!" Russell said. Then he softened. "I'm sorry, honey," he said, and came up and hugged her. Mary apologized too, and they parted on good terms.

But minutes after he was gone, Mary felt sad again. What was going on?

Sam was crying; it was time for dinner.

Russell picked up Kevin and drove him to the shanty in silence. When they arrived, Sheri was already at the bench, opening beside Mike.

"What are you doing here?" Russell asked Sheri, pushing ahead of Kevin. The suaveness was not in his voice now; his exasperation was finally beginning to show.

"I came to help," she said cheerfully. She had to

speak loudly. Mike had brought in a tape deck and was playing a Credence Clearwater tape at full volume.

"I wondered where you were. I thought I told you not to come," Kevin said.

"I'm doing fine," she said. "Mike has been a good teacher."

"Mike's only learning himself," Russell put in. "Look, I don't care which one of you does it, but I want to make sure you do it right. I don't want you cutting up my fish. Now come with me." He took Sheri and Kevin off to the side and gave them a lesson in opening. Sheri was slow at picking it up, but Kevin was unbelievably fast. Soon he was doing so well that it was clear Sheri was not needed, and she got ready to go home.

"Please be careful, Kevin," she said as she took off her plastic apron. "Don't hurt your hands."

"Why, are his hands worth a million dollars or something?" Russell commented.

"Didn't you know?" she asked Russell. "He's a concert violinist. He's played since he was three years old."

Russell just raised his eyebrows.

After Sheri left, Russell watched Kevin in silence a few minutes.

"You've never done this before?" Russell asked, a tone of grudging respect in his voice. He spoke loudly to be heard above the music.

"Not that I can remember," Kevin said, "and I think I probably would remember."

"Maybe all those years of playing violin will pay off," Russell said, with no irony intended.

"Your mother," Kevin replied.

"What?" Russell asked. "What did you say?"

Kevin looked up at Russell, who stood nearly a foot taller than him and weighed almost a hundred pounds more. He smiled, admitting but disarming his statement.

"Your mother should have made you take violin lessons too."

"I'll be back later to see how you're doing," Russell said.

"Don't worry," Kevin said. "I'll do 'em."

Russell looked as if he wanted to say something more; then his expression hardened and he left.

The Credence Clearwater tape started to repeat, and Mike took it out and put in a hard rock tape. Kevin grimaced. He endured the music in silence for a few minutes before he spoke up.

"Listen, Mike, you mind turning it down a little?" Kevin asked him.

"Yeah, I do mind," Mike said. He turned toward Kevin. His eyes had a wild, unfocused glare, like light reflecting off a globe of glass.

"Turn it down!" someone else shouted.

"What if I don't feel like turning it down?" Mike shouted back.

"Just do it!"

Mike reached over and turned it down, with an angry glance toward Kevin.

"Bastards," he muttered to himself.

Kevin, opening the scallops faster and faster, was soon outpacing Mike. Kevin opened two boxes and went on to a third, just out of momentum. When Russell came back later, Kevin had opened fourteen pounds in two hours. Russell watched as Kevin finished the third box.

"Not bad," Russell told him. "Now go on home, get some rest."

"Right."

"Let's make it a little later tomorrow: six thirty. Give us both a chance to rest up a little."

"Okay."

"Want a ride?"

"No. I'll walk."

The sky had cleared. The moon, more than three quarters full, rode low in the east, perfectly clear. Low in the west, Venus burned greenish yellow. Orion was climbing in the east. A falling star streaked across the heavens and disappeared behind the roof of a house.

Kevin saw the beauty of the scene without feeling it. He felt, suddenly, exhausted.

When he came home Sheri was in one of her concerned moods.

"You know I only went there because I didn't want you to hurt your hands," she said, with a mixture of apology and reproach. A scarf was around her hair; Kevin had noticed that she tied a scarf around her head when she felt the need to apologize about something.

"I didn't hurt my hands," he said.

"You won't be opening any more, will you?"

"I don't know. It might turn out to be a pretty easy way to make money."

"Please don't," Sheri said. "Remember what you're here for."

"What am I here for?"

"Kevin, don't talk like that."

"No, sometimes I wonder," he said. "I wonder what the hell I'm doing here, on this crummy little island."

"You came here to play violin. You have an audition soon."

"No, you have it all backwards," he said. "I played violin so I could prepare to be the world's greatest scallop opener."

Sheri looked at him, and something in her face changed. Kevin thought she realized he had bested her. But Sheri was thinking of another attitude toward hardship, a quiet, stoic cheerfulness that she knew and respected, though for a moment she didn't picture the person who embodied it.

"Aunt Maude called while you were at the shanty," she said. "There's a meeting about the church tonight. She asked me to go. Would you like to come?"

"No, that's okay."

"All right, see you soon." She kissed him goodbye and left.

As Sheri walked out into the night air, she realized how little she had seen her great-aunt since Kevin arrived that fall. She promised herself to visit Maude more often. Maude had lung cancer; after months of chemotherapy her condition was not improving. Although she was weaker, she maintained the clarity and force of mind that had attracted and intimidated Sheri since she was a little girl. Sheri knew Maude must have noted her absence.

Sheri wended her way through the small back streets, steering toward the floodlit four-faced clock tower of South Church. She came to the front of the building and pulled at one of the massive double doors; it stuck, and she had to use all her strength to wrench it open. Quietly, she made her way up the winding stairs. The meeting was already in progress, and Sheri walked with bowed head into the cold hall. About seventy people were huddled in the first several rows; more than two thirds of the hall was empty. In the last occupied row, Sheri found a seat next to Maude, who looked over at her and nodded.

Maude had aged noticeably even in the few weeks since Sheri had last seen her. Her face was paler and shrunken and looked far older than her seventy years. Her eyes were still alert, but they had a detached, watchful expression that was new. Sheri reached over and took her hand, and Maude signaled with her eyes that Sheri should pay attention to the speaker in the front of the room.

A large, bald-headed gentleman with striking eyebrows was addressing the congregation. He was saying that the church was in need of extensive renovation, perhaps structural as well as cosmetic, and he confirmed the rumor that a Boston developer by the name of Woolsey had offered to purchase the church for his own use. In addition, Woolsey proposed to build a smaller meetinghouse for the congregation on a site yet to be determined at the edge of town. As the details were explained, Sheri felt a silence forming in the room.

The speaker paused a moment, looking down at his notes. Then he looked up. "I think we all recognize the fact that this offer would solve several problems we currently face."

He stopped again, as though waiting for a reaction. A second later, Maude's voice, low but distinct, rose from the pew.

"I think it would cause a hell of a lot more problems than it would solve."

Her statement was greeted by a few grunts of agreement and then, an instant later, by loud applause. People turned in their seats, smiling and nodding. Sheri became aware of Frank, seated next to his wife in the front pew.

The large man at the front of the room went on to say that it was the unanimous—he stressed this word, and several people near the front nodded their heads— the unanimous recommendation of the trustees that the offer be rejected. However, a renovation fund would have to be established if the present church building was to remain in use. A huge sum would be needed:

$500,000 or more. Everyone would have to help in the fund-raising effort.

A vote was taken, by show of hands, to begin as soon as possible. A committee was chosen to oversee the fund drive.

As the meeting continued, Sheri looked around the room. It was a deep, high hall with long leaded windows along either side. In the rear were the choir loft and organ; in the chancel at the front were the Wendte trompe l'oeil paintings that gave the illusion of three-dimensional columns. Overhead were more trompe l'oeil paintings, giving the appearance of ceiling panels. The pews were hand-carved mahogany, with scarlet cushions.

As Sheri looked closer, she noticed gaping cracks in the ceiling plaster, flaking paint on the vestibule wall, holes cut in the plaster near some windows to assess structural damage. Clearly, there were serious problems. Yet despite these problems, or perhaps because of them, she sensed a strong resolve in the people around her.

Although Sheri had enjoyed attending church as a girl in her hometown in Connecticut, since going away to college she had thought of church as a basically unalive thing—an excuse to dress up on Sunday and socialize. The combination of frailty and resolve in the room challenged that belief.

Near the end of the meeting the minister, a man as long and lean as a razor-clam shell, stood up to speak. He said that what they were attempting to do would be perhaps the greatest challenge the church had ever faced. He thought it could be done, but it would require enormous effort by everyone. He thanked them all for coming. The meeting ended quietly and with an air of doubt.

54

"Well, what do you think of our island affairs?" Maude asked Sheri in her low, throaty voice. A faint odor like dried wood seemed to come from her skin.

"Can the congregation do it?" Sheri asked.

"If they want to."

"They seem determined enough."

"They were on a high. But they're coming down. They'll all go home and realize how much work is ahead of them. Well, look at this! Here comes my boyfriend," Maude said, her pale blue eyes looking directly ahead. Frank, followed by Suzanne, was making his way down the hall with his typical shuffling gait. There was still a trace in his walk of his leg injury from a fishing accident years earlier.

"Good evening, ladies," he said. Maude reached out and took his hand.

"Are you taking good care of my niece on that boat of yours?" she asked him.

"Oh yes," he said, rubbing his dimpled chin and winking at Sheri. Suzanne came up beside him, and Frank introduced her to Sheri.

"We're looking forward to dinner tomorrow night," Suzanne said.

"I'm glad you can come," Sheri said. She saw something open and warm in Suzanne's face and manner that attracted her.

"Well, we'd best be going. Can't keep the other guys waiting," Frank said.

"The boys rehearsing tonight?" Maude asked.

"Every Thursday," Frank said.

"Remember what I asked you the other day."

Frank shook his head and narrowed his eyes. "Now, it's too early to talk about that, Maude."

"It isn't. And I want one of the pretty ones, like 'Aura Lee.'"

"Darling, we'll give you whatever you want," Frank said. Then he was gone, with Suzanne at his side.

Sheri looked over at her aunt with a questioning glance.

"His barbershop group is going to sing for me," Maude said.

"Oh? I didn't know he had a group."

"He has a wonderful voice, didn't you know that?"

"No."

"I've always had a crush on that man. He's the younger man in my life. Of course, he must seem hopelessly old to you."

"Not so old."

"He's always reminded me of your father—his singing. Your father was my favorite nephew, I'll have you know. I loved his voice too."

"He had a wonderful voice."

"There are definite similarities between the two men. The same impatience with the world."

"Frank doesn't seem impatient."

Maude waved her arm. "Young people don't know what patience is. Come visit me when you have a chance. Now I have to get home to bed." She called to her nurse, who came over and helped her up. Sheri walked alongside.

"There's something special about this church," Sheri said.

"What's special?"

"I don't know for sure. A feeling of unity, I think."

"That's life out at sea," Maude said. "Where else does everyone in the community come to a baby's christening or to a small child's birthday party? That sort of thing is common here in the winter months." The live-in nurse helped lift her into the car. Sheri hovered nearby, waiting for something nameless. "Now go home and get some sleep," Maude told her. "I'm sure you don't sleep late these days."

"Goodbye, aunt." Was there something else she should have said?

On her way home she found herself thinking of her father. Clear as a reflection in still water, he took his place in her thoughts. He had died of a heart attack while Sheri was in high school. It happened during breakfast one morning; he slid from his chair and lay floundering on the floor, doubled up in agony, as she watched helplessly. She had never forgiven herself. Now she was a certified EMT; she had even trained Kevin in the rudiments. But somehow everything she did seemed too unimportant, too late. Sheri often wondered what her father would think of her now if he could see her. Would he be proud, worried, surprised, confused?

She tried to see the resemblance to Frank, but her mind wandered, and before she knew it she was back at the house on Pleasant Street. She went to bed. Kevin was already asleep.

Frank was over at Milton Coffin's house, singing in their barbershop quartet. Every Thursday evening the guys met down in Milton's basement, in a large recreation room that had once been a playroom for his children. The cement block walls had been left unfinished except for a coat of white paint, and the acoustics were echoey enough to hide the mistakes and make the close harmonies sound larger and fuller.

Gin and tonic was their drink, even in winter; it seemed to make them sing better, or at least gave them that illusion. When Frank arrived tonight the others were already there, and a gin and tonic was waiting for him.

"There he is, the old lecher," Jack said. He was a

printer for the *Inquirer and Mirror* and sang baritone in the group.

"Old lecher?" Frank asked, with a wink.

"I saw who you were talking to tonight after the meeting," Sammy said. Sammy, who was Suzanne's older brother, sang lead; he was the manager of a clothing store.

"She's my culler."

"Sure, sure. Just talking to her about fishing, were you?" Sam made a few fishlike movements.

"Going after a double limit, huh, Frank?" Jack put in.

"Aw, jeez," Frank said. "You guys. Just an innocent business partnership, that's all."

"Innocent, huh?" Milton asked. He had a high-pitched voice as hollow as the sound made by blowing across a soda bottle. It was a perfect first-tenor voice for barbershop.

"Yeah, 'fess up," Sammy said. "I got the virtue of my little sister to maintain." Sammy had high cheekbones, like Suzanne, but his jutting chin seemed to sum up the ways he differed from Suzanne. Where Suzanne was gentle and tactful, Sammy was blunt and assertive.

Frank looked Sammy square in the eye. His golden-brown eye had a very serious expression; the gray one seemed to look on neutrally.

"I admit it," he said. Milton whooped, and Jack choked on his drink.

"Admit what, Franky?" Milton's soda-bottle voice inquired.

Frank turned his palms upwards. "I tried, but I can't get it up any more."

The others whooped and hollered, even Sammy, who usually took himself too seriously to let down. They patted Frank on the back and punched him in the arm. Then, without warning, Frank launched into the low C that began "Coney Island Baby." One after another, they found their starting notes and rushed headlong into the melody.

> *Goodbye, my Coney Island baby,*
> *Farewell, my own true love.*
> *I'm gonna go away and leave you,*
> *Never to see you any more.*
> *I'm gonna sail upon that ferryboat,*
> *Never to return again.*

This was always their opening number, whenever they performed in public or for friends at parties. It always got a big laugh, in the place where the words were:

> *Then we join the army of married boobs,*
> *To the altar—*

and Frank sang the same solo every time, with his arms raised above his head:

> *Drop that gun! I'll marry your daughter!*

They were in good form tonight. Their voices rose and fell like waves, swooping and rolling. On their best nights it seemed to Frank that the group was like the crew of a well-run ship. Sammy's clear, true lead was the captain, tracing a steady course through the song. Milton's first tenor was the lookout, following the direction set by the captain but calling out changes in course. Jack's baritone was an ironic undercurrent, just beneath the captain, like the mumbling of a slightly dissatisfied but competent crew. And Frank's bass was the roll and tumble of the ocean, imparting a sense of rhythm and urgency.

Milton was Frank's best friend in the group, and probably his best friend overall. Jack was a little too sarcastic for him, and Sammy a little overbearing, but Milton and he got along fine. Milton was always good-natured, always glad to see Frank and concerned about him. Milton didn't seem to care much about himself. He was like Suzanne in that way, though Frank had never thought much about that.

When they finished "Coney Island Baby," Milton said, "So, Franky, you gonna hop on that ferryboat with your young lady? You gonna run away?"

Frank shrugged his shoulders and made a face. As far as he was concerned, the subject was closed. And if the others wanted to stay on his good side, they would forget it too.

"So, I understand Woolsey is trying to buy your church, turn it into a mall," Jack said, in the dry, sarcastic way that suggested he was somewhat detached from this frivolity.

"Where'd you hear that?" Milton asked.

"Down at the paper," Jack said. "They're saying he's offered plenty, and he doesn't ever expect to recoup more than a third of it. But he thinks Nantucket needs an indoor shopping area, and there's no other place downtown where it could go."

"We won't let him," Milton said. "We had a meeting about it tonight."

"He already owns a few buildings downtown," Sammy said, and a scowl came over his face. "Why doesn't he knock one of 'em down and build a mall there?"

"Historic Districts Commission would never allow it," Jack said. "Besides, he makes money on those buildings. But if he buys your church, he can take a loss on it and write it off." Jack was the only Catholic among them; the rest were members of the Second Congregational Meeting House Society, which was the official name of South Church.

"He can't buy it unless we let him," Milton said. "And we won't."

Jack shrugged. "Then you better raise a lot of money fast. From what I understand, your church needs a lot of work. Damn thing's about to fall down."

Sammy scowled again. "Woolsey should give us the money, instead of trying to buy the building from us. He just wants to control the whole island, like others before him."

"Well, now, wait a minute," Jack said. Perhaps because of his Catholicism, he considered himself the freethinker of the group. "The commercial interests have done a lot for this island. They refurbished a lot of the inns back when they were nothing. The Looms only got set up because they brought weavers over for the inns. And now that skill has spread to natives like Suzanne, to everyone's benefit. The whole downtown area would be nothing without people like Woolsey."

"He's just protecting his investments, making improvements that raise their value," Sammy said, still scowling.

"I admit, that's part of it," Jack said, waving his gin and tonic around in a speculative way. "But he's got to care about the island too, or he wouldn't put so much into what he does."

"I might feel different if he really lived here. At least some of the other big guys, they live here year round; their families live here. But Woolsey lives up in Beantown and only comes for a month or two in the summer."

There was a silence for a few moments.

"Jeez, we wouldn't let him buy the church, would we?" Milton asked. "Even if we couldn't raise the money, we wouldn't let him do that, would we?"

No one answered.

"I better be going," Frank said. "Gotta get up early these days." He finished his drink.

"Franky, we hardly sang," Milton complained.

"Next time, guys. We got off to a late start tonight."

"Remember, we're singing at a party for Russell and his wife Sunday afternoon," Jack said. "Their little Sammy is a year old."

"That's how old our little Sammy is too, isn't that right, Sammy?" Milton asked. But no one picked up on his attempt at humor.

Frank walked outside, into the mild November air. The stars were brilliant. The moon, nearly full, had climbed high in the east. There was a ring around it; bad weather was on the way.

CHAPTER 5

For most of their married life, Suzanne had been Frank's culler; she had stopped just a few years earlier. But she still got up with Frank each morning and fixed his breakfast. She loved the early morning, the quiet, and the peace of being alone in the kitchen before anyone else was about. She would bring the room to life with the breakfast smells and sounds—bacon sizzling in the skillet, potatoes frying in the pan, toast crisping in the oven. To preserve the delicacy of the morning, she never turned on the overhead fluorescent light but worked by the faint glow of a tiny reading lamp on the table, which allowed her to witness the trees taking shape against the eastern sky. By the time Frank came downstairs, there was a rosy gleam on the side of the shed out back, and the dew sparkled blue and green.

Frank ate quickly, and there was almost never any conversation. But by the time he left, the daylight was pale and full. By then, her tiny lamp cast only a faint circle on the table. She would wash the dishes, sit down again for a cup of coffee, and watch the world unfold. Goldfinches hopped around on the feeder outside, their summer brilliance reduced to pale yellow; a V of Canada geese swept by, on their way to Cisco Beach to feed for the day; the calico cat prowled the yard, with a lazy mime of vigilance. This was Suzanne's favorite time of day, when she could just sit still and watch and let her mind wander where it would.

But on Friday morning, her thoughts were disturbed. Although she tried not to dwell on it, she was bothered that Sheri was on the boat with Frank. She pictured them out on the water and wondered if the Horseshed would be crowded, as Frank had predicted. She wondered what the other scallopers thought of Sheri. Her musings wandered then to Russell and to Roger and then to her son, Mike. She had heard about the run-in between Roger and Mike. She sat over her cup of coffee longer than usual that morning, and she was still disturbed when she finally went over to the loom to get to work.

As Frank had predicted, the Horseshed was bristling with boats. The word had finally gotten around, and perhaps forty of the total fleet of a hundred boats were there. It was a drizzly, sloppy morning. Boats crisscrossed back and forth, sometimes catching each other's lines. At the end of the tows, as the boats stopped to cull, conversations started between the different crews.

Russell spoke loudly and boisterously to the other boats. Caught with his hand in the cookie jar (as he put it to Kevin), he acted as though his goal all along had been to find a spot he could share with the others. Now that there was no denying how good the fishing was there, he gave the others explicit instructions on setting up for the best tow.

"Damn," he confided to Kevin, still smiling toward the other scallopers. "We've been found out!"

From time to time he glanced over and saw that Kevin was doing a better job at culling.

Different boats came up to them throughout the day. About noon they were joined by Roger, who scalloped alone. He set up a tow in Russell's wake and stopped just a few yards away to cull off his board.

"Hello, Roger," Russell said, in his most friendly tone. He remembered how he had talked down the Horseshed to Roger and was apologizing for it in his indirect way.

"Damn," was all Roger said in response. His hands flew on the culling board.

"You like?" Russell asked.

"I love, man. These are beautiful."

"Not bad, not bad. Not as junky as it was the other day. I cleaned it out for you guys."

Roger held up a toadfish. "If you strap one of these under the board, you can get one hell of a blow job," he said. "You should try it sometime."

"Oh, man, you're gross!" Russell said. "Isn't he gross, Kevin?"

"I think you would like his teeth," Roger said.

"Okay, okay, I get the point," Russell said. "Russell O'Grady is the bad guy, right? Is that it?"

"That's it," Roger agreed. He looked over and smiled his crooked grin.

Across the way, Frank was bringing in a tow while Sheri culled off the board. Russell waved to Frank and shrugged with a "What, me worry?" expression.

"That kid of Frank's is trouble," Roger said. "He pulled a scallop knife on me the other night."

"I know," Russell said. "I was there."

"If it wasn't for his mother, I'd show him a thing or two. But she stopped me on the street yesterday and asked me to hold off. I wouldn't do it for anyone but her."

"Suzanne is a sweetheart," Russell replied.

"Still, if he tries any more monkey business, I'm going to let him have it."

"Don't take him seriously, Roger. He's just a kid."

"I don't know how a woman like her could have a son like that."

"Aw, come on, Roger. You probably had a nice mother, too."

Roger paused a minute, but by the time he understood the insult, Russell had cranked up his motor and was headed back to the start of the tow. He made a face at Roger and bit his thumb. Grim-faced, Roger shook his head and went back to his culling.

Frank, eyeing the other boats, was shaking his head. "I think it's time for us to take a little trip to Tuckernuck," he said.

"The island?" Sheri asked.

He didn't answer.

"Are there scallops there?" she asked, letting him know that she would not be dismissed in silence.

"Best in the world," he replied, in a voice that suggested everyone in the world knew that. Then, by way of explanation, he said, "Tuckernuck has a good strong tide, stronger even then the Horseshed. And cleaner water, away from town."

"It looks like a pretty place," she said. "I've never been there, but I've seen it from shore, from Madaket."

Again he didn't reply. He started up the donkey and began to bring in another tow. As he turned his back, Sheri stuck her tongue out at him. Just then, Kevin and Russell pulled up alongside. Feeling that she had made a fool of herself, Sheri bent closer over the culling board.

The steady rhythm of the day continued: throw out the dredges, pull them back in, cull off the board, throw out the dredges. On and on. Frank made eighteen tows before the tenth box was finally filled. His arms were heavy and his breath was short by that point, though he said nothing.

He took just one break, when he drank a small can of tomato juice. As usual, he tossed the empty can into the water. Sheri had been shocked the first time she saw him do this—think how dirty the water would become if everyone acted that way! But the more she thought about it, the more it seemed all right for Frank to do it. He had grown up on the water before there were a lot of summer people and yachts fouling up the harbor; it was part of his heritage to think that the water could absorb litter. But she would never throw a can into the water herself.

During all this time neither of them spoke. Sheri found herself immersed in the process of scalloping, seeing how many baskets each new tow would fill. She knew that Frank was trying some different things: one tow was twice as long as the others, one went in a new direction. But she didn't ask him, as she normally might, about what he was changing. She simply culled off the board, again and again and again.

They came back to town and lifted the boxes up onto the dock. The clock on South Church tower said three thirty. It was the latest they had come in yet.

Sheri helped Frank put the boxes in the back of his pickup truck. On the first day of the season, she had barely been able to lift a full box. Now, although it was still a strain, she could do it. It wasn't that she was stronger so much as that she had a better idea of how to use her body—to lift the box by swinging it forward so that its own momentum helped to carry it up.

A short, dark man was watching her. She had seen him there before and didn't like his presumptuousness.

He strolled up to the truck, nodded curtly at Frank, and strolled away.

"Who was that?" Sheri asked when he was gone.

"That's Charlie. The warden," Frank replied.

"Oh."

"Yep, that's Charlie, all right. Checking for seed and making sure we didn't crown up the boxes too high. He didn't like the look of these today; we'd better make sure we flatten them out a bit from now on."

"You mean put less in?"

"Naw. Put the same amount in, but shake 'em down so it looks like less."

They climbed into the truck.

"Umm-huh. There's all sorts of tricks to fit more in a box. Some guys take their boxes home and put 'em in a hot bath and stretch 'em out with a stick. All sorts of tricks."

"Is it all right if I don't help you unload at the shanty today?" Sheri asked. "I'd better get home and start dinner."

"Got a hungry man to feed tonight?"

"Several," Sheri said.

"Several?" Frank asked.

"I hope they're hungry," she said.

Frank raised his eyebrows and started the engine. He dropped Sheri off at the corner of Main and Pleasant.

"See you tomorrow, same time," he said.

"See you tonight," Sheri corrected him.

"Tonight?"

"Didn't you know? You and Suzanne and Russell and Mary are coming over for dinner tonight."

"We are?"

"Didn't Suzanne tell you?"

"Wait a minute." A look of genuine concentration

came across Frank's weathered face. "Come to think of it, maybe she did tell me. How about that. Hmph."

"Just don't forget to come," Sheri said with a playful lilt in her voice which felt somehow wrong to her even as she spoke. She walked off down the street, feeling his eyes on her.

Sheri barely had dinner ready at seven that night when the guests arrived. Russell and Mary came first, with Sam. Russell had on a jacket and tie and was carrying a bottle of wine under his arm.

"A little present. For you," he said. Sheri had on a simple black dress, cut just below the shoulders, with a string of pearls around her neck. The outfit accentuated her dark hair and eyes and set in fine relief her straight, chiseled features. But she felt uncomfortable when she saw Mary's simple blouse and skirt: even allowing for the fact that Mary was wearing maternity clothes, Sheri realized she was overdressed by the standards of the year-round community.

Kevin stood beside her, maybe half an inch shorter, looking a little stiff and uncomfortable. He nodded his head in his usual way and peered out from behind his wire-rimmed glasses. He had on a white shirt and dark pants held up by suspenders.

"Kevy! I love those suspenders!" Russell said, coming over to him. "I've been trying to get me a pair of those, but Mary says I can't."

"These men! They're just like peacocks," Mary said, with a soft voice that was confident of silencing her louder, larger husband.

"Me? I'm not a peacock!" Russell said. He appealed to Sheri. "Do I look like a peacock?"

Sheri opened her mouth to reply and then closed it, as if the truth might be too painful.

"Very funny!" Russell said, as Mary broke into a peal of laughter, more in criticism of her husband than in appreciation of Sheri's sense of humor. He picked up Sam and carried him over to a sofa. "Come on, Sam, you're the only one here that likes your poor dad." Sam squirmed away and ran across the floor toward Kevin. He stopped a few feet away and stood staring. "I take that back," Russell said.

Suzanne and Frank arrived a few minutes later. Suzanne came in first, carrying a covered dish. She was wearing a shawl, one of her own, of warm brown and dusky gray; it set off her blue eyes and dark hair, parted to the side. Frank came in behind her, in gray slacks and a white shirt open at the collar. He looked embarrassed and ill at ease, out of his element.

Sheri walked up to Suzanne and took her hand. "How lovely," she said. "Where did you find such a beautiful shawl?"

"It was just sitting there on my loom one day."

"You made it?"

"You shouldn't look so surprised, Sheri; you'll make me think you have no faith in my abilities whatsoever."

"I've just never seen such a lovely shawl. May I touch it?"

"Yes, of course," Suzanne said, smiling.

Sheri thought the shawl made Suzanne look younger and prettier, but as she stepped up to Suzanne, the contrast in their ages was striking to the others.

Sheri turned to Frank. "So, Frank, you remembered."

"I remembered for him," Suzanne said. "Frank always forgets our social dates. But he never forgets to go out scalloping."

"I get paid for scalloping," Frank said.

Suzanne walked over to Mary. "How are things?" she asked.

"Oh, not too bad," Mary replied. "It's still scalloping season."

Suzanne sat down beside her and asked quietly, "Did you have a good dinner the other night?"

"Russell had to go back to the shanty and help open."

Suzanne's reaction was just a tightening of the muscles around her mouth, which only Mary could see. "That won't happen every night," she told Mary. Sam came over to her, and she tried to tickle him. Sam frowned and turned away.

"Shy tonight," Mary confided in a quiet voice. "Strange house, strange new people."

"But nice enough," Suzanne said to Sam, in a tone of voice which made Mary wonder if she really meant it.

Frank and Russell soon established themselves on the sofa and began to discuss the Horseshed and how long the scallops there would last. Frank was shaking his head; Russell had a long expression.

"You heading out to the West End?" he asked.

"I don't know; we may have no choice," Frank replied. Sheri came into the room with some beers and stopped to listen. Suzanne and Mary were listening too.

"Are you going to Tuckernuck tomorrow?" Suzanne asked Frank.

"Never can tell," Frank said, in a teasing tone. He looked over at Sheri and winked.

"Oh, these scallopers," Mary said. "So much mystery and intrigue."

"Frank's always been this way about scalloping," Suzanne announced in Sheri's direction. Her tone was unusually assertive, as though to demonstrate how well she knew him. "There have to be surprises every day."

"Just in scalloping?" Frank asked.

"No, honey, in everything," Suzanne obliged him.

Sheri offered them the beers. Frank accepted his, but Russell waved away the beer intended for him.

"No, thanks," he said.

"What can I get you?" Sheri asked. "We have wine and we have some Kahlua."

"A soda will be fine," Russell said.

Suzanne followed Sheri out into the kitchen. "Russell used to have a drinking problem," she explained, in her soft, musical voice. "That's why he wouldn't accept the beer."

"Oh," Sheri said. "I wish I'd known." She poured some ginger ale into a glass and waited for it to fizz down.

"You had no way of knowing. I'm just telling you so you understand."

Sheri turned to Suzanne. It seemed like one of those moments between two people when real friendship can take root, and she was eager for a glance that would confirm their shared intimacy. But Suzanne proved suddenly elusive. She became busy arranging a platter of vegetables and dip, and her conversation switched to trivial subjects—whether or not to scrape the skin off carrots, whether raw cauliflower causes heartburn. Her voice, normally so soft and musical, had become sing-songy. In a moment she was gone, carrying the platter out into the living room. Sheri had a sense that the gates had slammed shut, leaving her outside.

Sam had discovered Kevin, to the curiosity of each.

"Eye!" Sam said, pointing at Kevin's glasses.

"These are glasses," Kevin told him.

"Eye!" Sam repeated. Sheri watched from the doorway. She expected Kevin to be ill at ease around such a small child. But he seemed comfortable, though he did watch the child with a certain scientific dispassion.

When Sam walked, he still looked as though he were falling upward from step to step. He toddled over to Kevin and put his hands on Kevin's knees.

"Eye!" He pointed again at Kevin's glasses and stared at Kevin with glassy, watery eyes.

"No, glasses," Kevin repeated, keeping perfectly still and focusing totally on Sam, without regard to the others in the room, who were all watching. It was the same concentration he showed when he played violin.

"Eye!" Sam cried. He put one hand on Kevin's knee and reached for the glasses.

"No," Kevin said. "Don't touch."

Sam reached farther, and Kevin grabbed his hand and pushed it away, too hard and sudden.

Sam took a step back and fell, and a shocked expression came over his face. He began to cry.

Kevin looked around helplessly. Sam picked himself up and walked away, circling over toward Frank. Frank put down his beer and motioned to Sam.

"You can't touch his glasses, you rascal," he told Sam. "They might break. You don't want his glasses to break, do you?" Sam made an impatient, angry noise and Frank blew a raspberry at him. In a minute he had Sam laughing again. Sheri, still watching, thought how Kevin was stuck in one gear, how it held him away from other people. But Frank, for all his Yankee taciturnity, knew how to make contact.

Sheri walked back to the kitchen, and she heard Mary telling Kevin that he and Sheri should come to Sam's birthday party on Sunday evening. From the tone of Mary's voice, Sheri knew that Mary was trying to make Kevin feel better.

A few minutes later Sheri announced it was time for dinner. She stood in the doorway between the dining room and living room, looking as though she didn't know what to do with her elbows. Then she made a gesture that she knew was too broad, too theatrical. Everyone followed her into the dining room. Different courses of a buffet dinner were lined up along the table: salad, three kinds of vegetables, potatoes, and broiled scallops for the main course.

"Where'd you get these scallops?" Frank asked her, standing back beside her as Mary and Russell started down the line.

"I bought them at the shanty," she said.

"You shouldn't of done that. I would of given you as many as you needed."

"Oh," she said, nervously watching them taking the food.

"Every now and then a good culler deserves a bonus, you know."

She smiled at him and thought how handsome he looked, how boyish, with his round face and thick blond hair. Over the past few weeks he had grown long sideburns, all the way down to his jaw, and they accentuated the boyish look.

Sheri felt Suzanne beside her.

"Go on through first, honey," Frank told Suzanne.

"I can't wait to try the scallops," Suzanne said. "I'm always looking for new recipes for them."

"I hope you like them broiled," Sheri asked.

"Oh, yes," Suzanne said.

"Broiled, eh?" Frank said, in a doubtful tone.

"Don't you like them broiled?" Sheri asked.

"His all-time favorite is scallop stew, but he likes them broiled, don't worry," Suzanne said.

"I wish I'd known that," Sheri said.

"The stew is awfully rich," Suzanne said. "All butter and cream, and we're trying to cut down on his cholesterol." She started down the line. Sheri felt that Suzanne was being kind to her out of habit; she remained opaque and distant.

As they waited to go through the food line, Sheri and Frank tried to make conversation. They spoke about Heather's artwork, about how Sheri liked living on Nantucket, about Sheri's plans for the future. Frank initiated each of the topics with an observation, allowing Sheri to go on. But she just didn't know how to follow through on the conversation. She had a sudden sense that she didn't know Frank nearly so well as she had thought. Finally Frank and she were left alone by the food. He took her by the arm and made her go first. When they came into the living room with their plates, Russell was talking with more demonstrativeness and vigor than usual. Sheri was surprised to see that he held a beer securely in his right hand.

As the evening went on, Russell had another beer, and Sheri saw Mary give him some looks and finally say something to him. When he went out into the kitchen for a third beer, Mary raised her hands in futility. Suzanne got up and went after him, and Russell came back in with a sheepish grin on his face and a glass of ginger ale. But even two beers had affected him. He spoke loudly and too much. Toward the end of the evening he put his arm around Kevin and said, "You're gonna be all right, Kevy, you know that? You're gonna be all right."

Kevin gave him his noncommittal, assessing look.

"Don't look at me like that, Kevy. I like you, I really do. We're gonna get along just fine."

Mary exchanged a glance with Suzanne. She went into the other room and got all of Sam's things.

"Come on, Russell," she said.

"What? So early?" he asked, raising his glass of ginger ale.

"Let's go," she said, in a low voice

"She's making me go, Kevy," he confided to Kevin. "Whatta you think of that?"

"I think it's a good idea," Kevin said. "If you're planning to go out Saturday."

"You're damn right I am, Kevy," Russell said. "And tomorrow is Saturday, ain't it?"

"Yes, it is," Kevin said.

"I'll see you bright and early," he said. He let Mary lead him out through the door. Their voices floated back inside. He was protesting to her that he could drive, but at a few words from her he was quiet.

"We had better go, too, I guess," Suzanne said. She walked up to Sheri. "Thank you so much. We had a lovely time."

Her eyes were still evasive, and Sheri realized that Suzanne didn't trust her.

"Goodbye," she replied. "Thank you for coming." She wanted to say something more to Suzanne, something to bridge the gap between them; but she just took Suzanne's hand. Then she said goodbye to Frank, who winked at her in a fatherly way. She winked back, knowing as soon as she did so that it was somehow inappropriate; she was aware that Kevin was watching her, and she blushed. The door shut, leaving Kevin and her alone in the house.

"Am I just imagining it, or was that an awful party?" she asked, speaking more rapidly than usual.

"It was fine," Kevin replied. She couldn't gauge his reaction, but she suspected he had sensed something funny in her behavior.

"Do you really think so?"

"Great food," he said, turning away. "Too bad Russell started drinking. Got a little sloppy there."

"You really think the evening was all right?"

"Would I lie to you?" he asked.

Sheri knew the dinner had been a failure. The food had been fine, the conversation had been pleasant enough, but something was wrong. There was an awkwardness in the air that had gotten in the way of everything.

She stayed up late, cleaning up. Kevin was practicing in the living room. She thought of asking him to help and then just finished the dishes herself. As she worked, she found herself thinking of the times Frank had ignored her questions earlier in the day. It really peeved her. When Kevin came in later, he found her sponging off the counters and talking to herself.

"What's up?" he asked.

"Nothing," she replied. "I'm just upset about the party."

"It wasn't really that bad. You coming to bed?"

"I'll be there in a minute."

She stayed up a while longer, and when she finally went to bed Kevin was already asleep. She lay down on her side and rolled away from him.

CHAPTER 6

The next morning when Sheri walked over to Frank's house, Suzanne was outside, putting something in the back of the truck.

"Hi, Sheri. We'll be ready for you in just a minute," she said, in that artificial, singsongy tone that seemed designed to keep Sheri away. Sheri felt a flush of pride in response. As Suzanne came around to the front, Sheri got into the truck before her. It wasn't totally conscious, but it meant she would be seated between Frank and Suzanne.

Seeing Sheri there, Suzanne walked all the way around to the driver's side and slid across to the middle of the seat. Sheri felt herself bristling. She was at the age where a wife's claims on her husband seem dishonestly come by; and yet, at the same time, a wish was growing within her to settle down with a husband and raise a family.

"We really enjoyed dinner last night," Suzanne said. She gave no sign of feeling any hostility or threat, and Sheri wondered if she had been imagining it. Glancing at her now, Sheri thought Suzanne looked old and tired.

"I was so glad you could come. Are you going out with us this morning?" she asked.

"No," Suzanne said. "I'm just taking the truck, so I can pick you up later at your new location. I guess you two are going to the West End today. You'll dock in Madaket tonight, since it's closer."

"The West End?"

"Tuckernuck."

Frank came outside, limping slightly as always, carrying his thermos and a bag lunch. He put them on the floor on the driver's side and sat down behind the wheel, with a stiff, angular motion of his body. He rubbed his chin, cocked his head at an odd angle, and started up the motor.

"All set, honey," Suzanne told him. "The new bucket and oar are in the back."

"Umm-huh," Frank replied. "Good morning," he said to Sheri.

"Are we going to Tuckernuck?" Sheri asked.

"Yep, Tuckernuck," he said. Sheri noticed that he pronounced it differently from Suzanne.

"Is it *Tuck*ernuck or Tucker*nuck*?" she asked.

"I always say Tucker*nuck*," Frank told her. "That is, if I'm in the mood."

Sheri felt a change in her stomach then, and was sure it came from Suzanne's response to the way Frank spoke to her.

"You can say it either way, Sheri," Suzanne said. "Most people say *Tuck*ernuck."

It was quiet as they drove toward the boat, until Suzanne finally broke the silence.

"I didn't get much chance to talk to you last night, Sheri. How do you like scalloping?" She looked straight ahead as she spoke.

"I like it," Sheri said.

"Some people don't; they think it's too repetitive."

"A lot of things that involve repetitive motions are fun," Sheri responded, blushing a moment after she spoke.

"It is fun, isn't it? It really gets in your blood, and you can't stand to be away from it. You want to know where everyone is each day and what they caught." The longing in Suzanne's voice made it beautiful.

"I like being out on the water," Sheri replied, feeling a sudden surge of sadness as she looked at Suzanne's small, gentle face beside her.

The truck rumbled down the cobblestones and turned off onto the narrow brick road that took them past the Gazebo and Straight Wharf restaurant, both closed for the winter. They stopped at the Hy-Line dock. Sheri and Suzanne stood there in silence, waiting for Frank to bring the boat around from the boat basin.

"What's that?" Sheri exclaimed. A large shape, fully four feet across, had surfaced only a few yards from them, gray and smooth as elephant skin.

"That's a skate," Suzanne replied, as it sank away before them. "I didn't know they came all the way into the harbor."

"It's huge!"

"Some fishermen catch them and dice the meat and sell it as scallops," Suzanne added.

Frank brought the boat up beside the dock, and he and Sheri put the new bucket and oar and the empty boxes into the boat, and Frank lifted in two extra cans of gasoline. Suzanne stood beside the truck in silence, waiting until they were ready to go. Frank started up the motor and pulled out of the slip. He turned toward Suzanne with a wave and a funny little grin.

"What time?" she called to him.

"Oh, I guess we'll do a little exploring out there," Frank said. "I'd say about three."

"Okay. Just give me a call if you get in any earlier," Suzanne replied. She stood on the dock and waved as they slid away into the early morning. There was a low, thick bank of clouds in the east. As Suzanne watched, a thin line burst into yellow flame along the top; then a small piece of the sun appeared, too bright to look at directly. She turned away, and a small piece of scallop-shaped darkness danced in front of her eyes.

A few boats were already at the Horseshed. They waved as Frank went by, and Frank responded with just the slightest nod of his head, as though hoping to remain invisible. They cruised out through the jetty and turned west, following the Nantucket shoreline toward Tucker-nuck.

It was a clear, calm day. There were only small, barrel-like swells in Nantucket Sound, which is the 30-mile stretch of water between Nantucket and Cape Cod. Sheri had heard about how rough the sound could become—how it was perilous for small craft—but she had trouble picturing that now. The blue, sparkling water surrounded her with a sense of well-being.

They made steady progress along the Nantucket shoreline. From the water everything on shore appeared in miniature. A cable television antenna, a metal tower with a flat rectangle perched diagonally at the top, looked like a dentist's mirror. A satellite dish resembled a foghorn. The houses along the shore had the neat, quaint look of an artist's rendering.

Superimposed on the scenes, Sheri occasionally saw quick glimpses of her father: playing ball with her as a little girl, driving her to her first dance, lying on the kitchen floor. . . .

A dark spot on the water ahead marked Tucker-nuck. As they came steadily closer it began to resolve into shore and hills, with a few houses clustered on the largest hill.

"Does anyone live there?" Sheri asked Frank above the roar of the motor, which was nearly at full throttle.

"Only in summer," Frank said. "Years ago people lived there year-round."

"Have you ever lived there?"

Frank shook his head. "My grandfather grew up there. My sister uses the house in the summer."

Frank slowed down as they approached a large shipwreck. This wreck marked the first of the shoals to the east of Tuckernuck. The bottom was clearly visible, and care had to be taken to avoid running aground. Frank veered to the north, into deeper water. Following a circuitous course, they weaved their way through a series of shoals and came to the scallop bed off the eastern shore of Tuckernuck.

At their arrival, a flock of swans lifted heavily into the sky with a dazzling white shimmer of wings and formed a V, their long white necks fully extended. Frank cut the motor, and the sweep and squeak of their wings was clearly audible even as they gained height and speed. Sheri watched until they circled far over the island and disappeared.

"Quite a sight," Frank said.

Sheri felt too moved to answer. The sight had changed her image of swans forever, from something that belonged on cards with pink hearts to creatures of immense strength and majesty.

"Umm-huh," he said, as if agreeing with something she had said, and threw the first dredge into the water.

It was a hard day. The adult scallops were large and easy to spot, but they were obscured by a tremendous mass of small seed scallops that had to be pushed over the side. When they stopped for lunch, Sheri already felt that the day should be over. But they only had six boxes.

Eating her sandwich, she looked about and was struck by the sense of open space around them. In the town harbor she had always been conscious of buildings and people, but now there was only open water and one small, low island. Without the clock on the church tower, there wasn't even a way of knowing what time it was.

"Yep. I think I'll try a spot a little farther to the south after lunch," Frank said. "See if we can't find a few more adults. All these tows are wearing me out. I'm not as young as I once was, you know." His eyes glittered as he spoke, as if gauging her reaction.

He reached down under the culling board, pulled out a scallop knife, and opened one of the scallops.

"Here," he said, handing it to Sheri on the half shell. "See what you think of this."

It was pure white and larger even than the scallops from the Horseshed. Sheri raised the shell to her lips and tipped the eye into her mouth. It was delicious. It had a fresh, sweet, buttery taste that wasn't at all fishy. It was like the essence of the sea, the life-giving sea. Frank saw by her look that she liked it, so he handed her another and then, smiling, another.

They had no better luck after lunch. When they finally finished, it was quarter to four. The tide had been falling rapidly all afternoon, and long exposed stretches of sand lay around them, covered by feeding seagulls.

"We better head back," Frank said. "Before there's no water left at all."

He steered to the east, away from Tuckernuck, to skirt one sandbar, and then swung back to the south. He came in closer to shore, inside the shoals, and opened the throttle all the way. Sheri squatted down to level off the top of the boxes, so they wouldn't look too full. She had leveled off about half of them when suddenly the boat slammed to a halt. The jolt sent Sheri crashing into the boxes in front of her. Scallops spilled out onto the floor; the motor raced crazily; Frank was swearing—they were stopped. Then there was silence.

"Ran her aground," Frank said. In the distance, seagulls squawked and cried.

The boat had jumped right over the edge of a shoal and landed on top of it. It was resting in just a few inches of water.

"This must be a new shoal," Frank said. "I sure as hell never saw it before." He bent over the back to look at the motor. "Damn. Bent the blade."

"Can I do anything to help?" Sheri asked.

"No, you just sit tight," Frank said. He leaned over the back with a hammer and a weight from a dredge and banged the propeller blade straight.

"That takes care of that," he said. "Now we have to figure out how we're going to get the hell off here." Sheri, listening to him, realized that she had never heard him swear until now. Apparently he reserved it for occasions that truly demanded it.

Frank climbed out of the boat and walked all the way around it, sloshing through the shallow water. He shook his head.

"Don't look too good, Sheri," he said.

"Can I help?"

"There ain't a lot we can do." He swore again.

As he spoke, Sheri became aware of a presence. She turned and looked behind her, and there it was; the full moon, round and pale, floated above the eastern horizon. The rippling tide, still falling, was rushing toward it, across a sea of silver-blue space. Empty scallop shells, old sticks, pieces of seaweed were carried with the tide, as though obeying the summons of some distant master.

The whole scene had an eerie beauty that made Sheri want somehow to participate.

She climbed over the side of the boat and lowered herself into the water near Frank. The tide pulled across her ankles as though trying to catch her and throw her down; she leaned into its force to keep from falling. Everything in the water looked oddly clear, as though magnified: specks of shells, hermit crabs, blades of sea grass—all in motion. The whole sea was in concert. Sheri had a sudden sense of how erotic the tide was, and then, despite her better knowledge, she immediately felt a wave of misgiving and suspicion toward Frank. Was this simply a modified version of the ran-out-of-gas trick? She glanced over at him. He was shaking his head and muttering to himself. He bent again and looked at the propeller, with a concerned expression on his face.

Ashamed of her doubts, Sheri turned away and eyed the bottom.

"Honey, get back in the boat," Frank said. "We can't do anything until the tide gets higher."

"I don't mind being out here," she said. She bent and picked up an empty scallop shell that was being pushed along by the tide. It was light orange with bold ridges. A tiny crab crouched within, eyeing her distrustfully.

The tide was still falling. The exposed sandbars grew longer and flatter, taking on a lambent, rosy sheen as the light faded. The sky darkened to a rich, deep shade of blue. But the moon grew brighter and brighter; it seemed to be drawing all the light of the world unto itself. It was the clearest, fullest moon Sheri had ever seen.

Seagulls left their feedings in the flats and rose one by one, taking wing toward some distant point in the sky above Tuckernuck. The few houses up on the hill looked silver gray in the moonlight, which already was strong enough to leave shadows under the cliffs at the edge of the island. The moors shone with a faint, waxen green—greener than during the day, as though the moonlight brought out the last traces of summer.

Sheri, swishing around in her boots, was transfixed and wished they could stay there forever, wished the scene she was witnessing would never end. As if in answer to her wish, Frank shook his head again. "I don't know if we're going to be able to make it back tonight."

"Why not?"

"Even if the tide rises enough to float us off, it'll be dark by then, and we'll have a hell of time keeping off the other shoals."

"We'll have the moon," she said, wondering why she was offering arguments when what she wanted was to stay, to stay.

"Not good enough," he replied. In a glance he took in the size of the sandbars, the depth of the water. "It's just stopped falling now." Half framed in the silvery light of the east and the pink afterglow of the west, his face seemed beautiful to Sheri—perfectly chiseled and articulated, like a statue. With his blond hair he seemed of no age, a perfect man.

"Where can we stay?" she asked, feeling an undertone of excitement coming into her voice and wondering if he sensed it.

"My sister's house," he said. "We're lucky this happened so close to shore. We'll have blankets and a wood-burning stove and beds. Nothing fancy, but we'll be warm. I'm sorry. I hope you don't mind."

"Oh, no," she said. "These things happen."

86

"Well, they're not supposed to. I thought I knew this shoreline; it's changing faster than I realized. It would help if I wore my glasses. I used to have better than twenty-twenty vision, but it's all started to go these past few years."

"I don't mind. Really." She could see he genuinely felt bad, and she wanted to say more to reassure him. Then something caught her attention.

"Look!" she said, taking Frank by the elbow and pointing. The V of swans was flying across the face of the moon, so close they could hear the creaking of their feathers and the rushing of the air. Their wings were silver and dark, rising and falling, and their long necks thrust forward, into the gathering darkness.

Frank anchored the boat and they sloshed through the hundred yards or so of water to shore. The western sky was charcoal gray now, and the only light was from the moon, which threw silver-gray shadows on the water in front of them. They came to the shore and struck a path that led past an old boathouse and up the hill to the houses. They walked through a long stretch of moorland, bayberry and scrub oak and other low bushes Sheri couldn't identify. It was quiet except for their footsteps. They didn't speak.

They walked past one house, then another, and finally came to the house that belonged to Frank's sister. The door lay in deep shadow.

Frank stopped before the door and rubbed his chin. "Umm-huh," he said.

Sheri felt a wave of affection for him.

Frank pushed the door open and found matches and an oil lamp on the kitchen counter. The flame flared up for an instant of full light which revealed old pine wainscoting, a delicate, spindly table and chairs, a large, deep sink. Then the flame burned down to a pale glow that caught their faces but left the details of the room in gloom.

Frank found some paper and kindling and started a fire in the stove. Light flickered through the grating. As her eyes adjusted to the room, Sheri became aware of a strange glow in another part of the room, over by the windows. She walked over to examine it. It was the moonlight, which fell in through the windows and lay on the floor like a finely woven carpet.

Once Frank had the stove going, she said, "If you tell me where the food is, I'll fix us some dinner."

He seemed surprised. "Just a can of beans is all I was thinking of, Sheri. You've had a long day."

"Let me see what I can do to make it a little more interesting."

He opened a cupboard for her, and she took out the cans and examined them. While he went down to the cellar to turn on the water, she concocted a mixture of green beans, mushrooms, canned chicken, and tomato sauce. While it was simmering in an old iron pan on the stove, she found dishes and set the table. Out of whimsy, she put two wineglasses by the plates. Then she returned to the stove and finished preparations for dinner. Frank came back into the room and rummaged around behind her. When she brought the food to the table, she was surprised to see a bottle of wine.

"I didn't think you'd have wine here," she said.

"You put out the glasses."

"What kind is it?"

"My sister's special Tuckernuck blueberry wine," Frank said. "To make up for all the inconvenience you've been caused."

"I've never had blueberry wine before." Sheri was conscious again of that undertone in her voice.

88

"It's something everybody should experience once in their life."

Sheri served the food and Frank sat down.

"Delicious." He sat there across from her, eating with obvious relish. After a minute he said, "Let's not forget the wine." He uncorked the bottle and poured out a glass for each of them. Sheri raised it to her lips and took a sip. The wine was sweet and acrid.

"Mmm. It does taste like blueberries," she said.

"Umm-huh," he said.

They ate in silence. Sheri finished her glass and poured herself another, remembering as she did so that she should have asked. But Frank didn't seem to mind. He seemed to be lost in thought. Sheri guessed what he might be thinking.

"I wonder if they're worried about us," she said. She certainly hoped Kevin was worried; if he wasn't, he was past being helped. As the wine went to her head, it seemed to her that Kevin deserved to be worried about her.

"Naw. Suzanne will know what happened. She knows it's a low tide tonight—always is on the full moon."

"It's too bad there's no way we can tell them we're all right."

"The only way would be to go back to Madaket, and then we wouldn't need to tell them."

Frank rarely said things like that, and this twisted piece of logic struck Sheri as quite funny.

"But we could send them a message in a bottle," she said, in a girlish, giggly tone. Then she felt embarrassed and fell silent.

"I used to be skipper of a sea-scalloping rig that stayed out for two weeks at a time," Frank said. "Suzanne didn't like it too much when I was away, but she understood. Sometimes we were out there in some pretty rough seas. She knows if I can handle that, I'm not going to get hurt in my own backyard in Tuckernuck."

This speech—so deliberate and factual—broke a spell that Sheri had fallen into. She had been constructing her own Frank in her mind, an all-knowing, romantic older man who had deliberately become shipwrecked with her on this remote island. As she realized what she had been doing, it was almost shocking, how much she had begun to believe in the fantasy.

By a parallel line of thought, Sheri wondered to what extent she had, all along, been constructing her own Kevin in her mind—someone who cared for her and was concerned about her more than the real Kevin was. This was just a passing thought, and not one she cared to dwell on for long. Instead, she poured herself another glass of wine.

"When did you start scalloping?" she asked.

"Bay scalloping?"

"Umm-huh."

"I started going out with my father on Sat'days when I was seven."

"When did you start going by yourself?"

"I must of been fifteen, sixteen. I still remember the first time I went out. I just had a little boat with a tiny little motor. I threw the lines out and I couldn't get the darn boat to move. I had a lot to learn."

"But you'd already been going out for eight years."

"Oh, I knew a lot about culling, but nothing about setting a tow. They were all laughing at me, all the other scallopers. Finally one of 'em comes over and asks if I'm planting potatoes. My warps were so long that my dredges were digging into the bottom. Plowing. I was some embarrassed, I can tell you that; all those men laughing at me. So I hauled back and shortened up the warps right away, and then I was okay."

Sheri got up and cleared the table. When she came back, Frank again seemed lost in thought. Made bolder by the wine, Sheri said, "What are you thinking about?"

Frank shrugged. "I was thinking about Mike," he said.

"Your son?"

"Yeah."

"He's been having a hard time recently?"

"That's an understatement. He's always getting in trouble. Always getting in fights."

"Why, do you think?"

"You know what it is—he's testing people. Seventeen years old and still testing people like a three-year-old."

"He doesn't seem like a bad guy."

"Oh, he can be nice enough. He can be a lot of fun when he wants to. But does he have a mouth! The only way to deal with him is to stand right up to him."

"He just hasn't had time to learn the difference between right and wrong," she said, trying to ease the weight on his mind.

"There is no right and wrong. It all depends on the culture. Different cultures have different rights and wrongs, and each culture has to be sure it teaches the children its own values. It all depends on how the culture defines them." He lapsed again into silence.

Sheri was surprised that Frank had thought so much about the subject, and she was surprised at his burst of articulateness. She looked shyly at her plate. Even if a fantasy had been dispelled, she did feel close to Frank; she felt as though she had known him all her life. Or was that simply another fantasy? Her mind couldn't focus; she couldn't be sure.

After dinner Sheri washed the dishes while Frank rummaged around for some blankets. He came back and motioned to her with his hand.

"Here," he said. She followed him. He held up an oil lamp. "This is the bedroom. Here's where you'll be sleeping." In a trim, wainscoted room was a single bed with an old metal frame.

"Okay," Sheri said. She was swaying slightly from the effects of the wine, and her arm brushed against his.

"There's plenty of blankets. If you leave the door open you should get warmth from the stove."

"I'm not worried about that."

He seemed a little embarrassed. "You could have the easy chair by the stove. That would be warmer, but I thought you might want a real bed. I'll take the chair, if that's all right with you."

"Fine," she said, with the sense that another fantasy was tumbling even before it had fully formed. But she had a sense that it hadn't become impossible, if it was what she wanted, which was something she couldn't seem to focus on.

She went back to the kitchen to finish cleaning up. Frank sat down in the easy chair by the stove and pulled a blanket over himself. Sheri wiped off the counter. "It really is lovely in this house. Your sister must love coming here in the summer."

Frank didn't answer. He was already asleep, with his mouth open. Something about his even, regular breathing made him seem childlike and lovable. At the same time, she was peeved that he had fallen asleep so quickly and easily.

Sheri cleaned up a little more and came over to stand by the stove. Frank was still asleep. She thought how good the warmth would feel on her skin. She pulled off her sweatshirt, her two sweaters, her boots. Then, knowing she was making a decision as she did so, she unbuttoned her shirt and pulled her undershirt over her head. She pulled off her pants and long underpants, then her socks, then her panty and bra. Her breasts and stomach took on an orange glow from the stove. Her nipples were erect from the combination of cold and heat. Goose bumps ran down her arms. She closed her eyes and ran her hands down her sides. She could feel the wine, or was she swaying from the motion of the boat all day? She thought she could feel moonlight on her skin. She had a sense that she was doing something utterly wicked, yet entirely innocent.

She turned, to warm her back, and wasn't surprised to feel the gentle touch of a hand on her shoulder.

"Umm-huh," she heard him say.

CHAPTER 7

All day Saturday, Russell was frustrated. After two days of being mauled by most of the fleet, the Horseshed was no good anymore. It wasn't that all the scallops were gone—he was pretty sure they weren't—but the bottom was fouled up. Instead of resting neatly on top of the mud, the scallops were all mixed up in it, like chips in chocolate ice cream. When the dredges came up they were filled with junk, so Russell was only getting about a basket a tow. By noon, he and Kevin only had four and a half boxes—after ten long, heavy tows. Russell was feeling it. This wasn't supposed to happen so early in the season. Or maybe it did happen every year, and he just couldn't remember from year to year.

To make matters worse, he had a dull headache—sort of like a hangover, though he only drank two beers the night before. Maybe it was just his nagging conscience: he knew he wasn't supposed to touch the stuff at all any more.

At the end of the next tow he cut the motor.

"How about some lunch, Kevin?" he said. Without replying, Kevin reached forward into the cabin and handed Russell his lunch, which was in a water-repellent foil bag. Russell unwrapped the turkey and cranberry sauce sandwich that Mary had made for him. Kevin opened a paper bag and unwrapped the ham and cheese sandwich that Sheri had made for him.

"Pretty heavy culling, huh?" Russell asked. Although he didn't comment on it, he had noticed that Kevin seemed a little faster and a lot more accurate these past two days.

"It isn't too bad," Kevin said. Looking at him, Russell realized that there was something about small people that fascinated him. They were so self-contained and tightly knit, they had such a remoteness about them. There was something intense about small people: whatever they thought, they thought it fiercely. And yet when it came down to it, what they thought didn't really matter, because they were small.

Still, he was beginning to develop a grudging respect for Kevin, the way Kevin had stuck it out the other night. Without quite thinking it through, Russell had been testing Kevin when he had him open those boxes. He could have found another opener for big scallops like that. But he had wanted to see how Kevin would react to pressure, and Kevin showed he could handle it.

Ever since then, Kevin had been quiet and distant— not impolite, but not exactly friendly, either. It was partly that he was concentrating on the work, that was clear. But something else was going on too, something Russell couldn't quite figure out. It intrigued him.

"What sort of music do you play on your violin, Kevin?" he asked.

Kevin shrugged. He opened his mouth to reply, but before he could speak, Russell went on.

"Beethoven, those guys?"

"Some of the later Beethoven quartets," Kevin said, with obvious restraint in his voice. "His concerto is a dud, though," he added with a little more naturalness. "Should have been left on the culling board."

"Who do you like?" Russell asked, his mouth full of turkey and bread.

"Most Bach, the Brahms concerto, Bartók."

"You practice a lot?"

"I try to get in four to five hours a day."

"Holy sheet! When do you find time for that?"

"After scalloping."

Russell thought this over a minute.

"I guess you can do that sort of thing if you don't have a family. But still, you got a girlfriend. Don't you spend any time with her?"

Kevin looked up with a slightly annoyed expression behind his glasses.

"She knows I need to practice," he said.

"Yeah, but doesn't she want a little company?"

"She's got things to do too."

"Four to five hours a day! I try to put in that much time on the house. But Mary would kill me if it was for any other reason."

Kevin didn't reply. Russell felt both stung, because he was beginning to want Kevin to be his friend, and annoyed, because as his employee Kevin should speak when spoken to. He frequently had this sort of ambivalent reaction toward Kevin: on the one hand he felt intimidated by Kevin's education and self-possession, and on the other hand, as Kevin's boss he knew he was far superior to Kevin in all aspects of scalloping. With other scallopers, Russell knew where he stood and felt comfortable with it; with Kevin, he wasn't sure. In the last few days, dealing with this uncertainty, he had adopted a brusque authoritarian tone.

"There's a lot you single guys don't understand," Russell said. "What it's like to have the demands of a family. My old friends wonder why I can't go out and have a drink with them any old time, like I used to. Last night was the first time in a couple years I've even had a beer. They just can't see the difference. They can't understand. It's crazy."

They ate in silence for a few minutes. Then, with the sort of quick decision that was characteristic of him, Russell decided to be friendly toward Kevin, as he had been during the first few days of the season. As soon as he made the decision, he found that he actually did feel more friendly toward Kevin, merely because he was addressing him as an ally and friend.

"That's a nice girl you got, Kevin," he said. "Excuse my asking, but have you two considered tying the knot?"

Kevin laughed. "I don't think either of us is ready for that," he said.

"Why not? You gotta do it sometime."

Kevin smiled and shook his head.

Russell, smiling back, said, "You find a nice girl, don't let her slip away. After my second date with Mary I asked her to marry me. I said, 'You look like the type of girl I'd like to settle down with and raise a family.' She turned me down every week for a year, and then, on the anniversary of our first date, she comes out and asks *me* to marry *her*. I tell you, I was one happy guy."

"Did it turn out okay? You didn't regret it?" Kevin asked, warming up despite himself to Russell's boyish display of openness.

"It's great! Hell, you know, sometimes we bark at each other, but I tell you, I'm at a happy period in my life. A family, a house—sometimes when I start to feel down about something, I step back and think about it and I can't believe my good fortune. Just can't believe it. Me, Russell O'Grady, with my own house and my own wife and kids."

A family and a house seemed more like encumbrances than assets to Kevin—but he found himself liking Russell because of the speech, there was something so undeniably good that shone through.

"I guess kids are okay," he said. "Sam's an interesting little guy."

"Fascinating," Russell said, breaking a brownie in two and handing half of it to Kevin. "Some of the things he does just kill me. He loves mud. He just loves it. He'll roll in a mud puddle any time he gets the chance—doesn't matter how cold it is. You've seen him, he's just a little guy, but he lets off some of the loudest farts you've ever heard, and what makes it even funnier is *he* thinks it's a riot, too. One time in the middle of the night, he let off this fart that shook the whole goddam apartment, and then this demonic laugh came from his room. And I swear to God, he had to be asleep the whole time."

Russell put the heel of his hand to his mouth and blew on it, to simulate the noise.

"Eating beans again, Russell?" a voice inquired.

"Oh, hi, Roger," Russell said.

Roger had cut his motor and glided up beside Russell's boat.

"I guess that's what they feed guys like you in the navy," he said.

"Navy? I ain't in the navy any more," Russell said. "What makes you think I'm still in the navy?"

"If you ain't in the navy, what the hell you doing with a PT boat?"

Russell smiled a big grin, to show he'd been had but didn't care.

"Hey, some guys may knock how she looks, but she's brought in more than a hundred and fifty thousand for me—clear—and that don't seem too bad. If they're doing better than that, they haven't told me about it."

"Some guys would rather starve than ride around in a PT boat."

"Yeah? Well, I say let 'em starve," Russell said, flushing, as the joke wore thin.

"Just kidding," Roger said. "Don't get mad. Hey, listen, big guy. You still want me to do that skim coat in your living room?"

"Yeah, sure," Russell said. "I can't pay much, though."

"No problem. When do you want me?"

"Well, how about tomorrow?"

"Tomorrow it is."

Russell suddenly became very excited. "Can you really do it tomorrow, Roger?"

"Sure, why not? I don't go to church."

"That's great! I'll hang the rest of the board this afternoon. That means we'll have it ready for Sam's birthday party! We can have the party in the new house!"

With a new burst of energy, Russell started up the donkey and hauled back the first dredge. Kevin set to work, pulling off the grass on top and tossing it over the side.

When Kevin got home late that afternoon, Sheri still wasn't in. This was unusual, but he thought little of it. He took out his violin and bow and stepped up to the music stand. He opened a book of Paganini studies and set it in front of the letter from Professor Blatt, which was still unopened.

One of the studies was a fast, gypsy-like piece with an inhumanly difficult section of ascending scales in thirds. Kevin worked on that part again and again, first slowly and precisely, then *a tempo*. But although he solved the intonation problems of the double stops, he couldn't get the section to flow. It continued to sound like separate bits of notes, each perfectly formed but with no smooth, inevitable progression.

Kevin sensed that something was wrong, but he couldn't pinpoint the problem. He played it again and again, until through sheer force of will he thought it sounded all right.

An insistently ringing phone interrupted his practice. Grudgingly, he went into the kitchen and picked up the receiver.

"Kevin?" It was a soft, musical woman's voice.

"Sheri?"

"It's Suzanne Hussey. I'm a little concerned because Frank isn't home yet. Have you heard anything from them?"

"No, I haven't," he said.

"Well, they're probably okay, but it's pitch dark outside, and I've called the shanty and there's no sign of them there either. They should be home by now."

"What could have happened to them?"

Suzanne heaved a sign. "It's a full moon tonight. That means the low tide is really low. They could have run aground on one of the shoals by Tuckernuck. But Frank knows those like the palm of his hand."

"Could it be engine trouble?"

"Maybe, but I doubt it. It's a new engine, and he just changed the plugs a few days ago." She sighed again. "Well, I guess we'll just have to sit tight and wait. I wouldn't worry. There isn't anyone who's better out on the water than Frank."

Kevin sensed that Suzanne was not worried about whether they were okay, but about something else.

"Let me know if there's anything I can do," he said.

"I will. Don't worry. I'm sure they're just fine."

Kevin walked back to the music stand and stood there a moment looking at the music, but he couldn't concentrate. He put away the violin and music. The letter was uncovered once again on the music stand. On a sudden impulse, Kevin sat down and opened it. He was expecting another short note. But instead, he was greeted by a long, single-spaced letter, painstakingly typed on an old manual typewriter, with half of the 'm' missing and the middle of the 'e' gone.

Dear Kevin,

Once more I implore you: come back to school. There is nothing disreputable or shameful about becoming a musicologist, to use your word. I prefer the term teacher. We need minds like yours. You could become a fine teacher, given a little more maturity and a sense of your place in the larger picture.

You think I can't see your profound need to be a great artist. But let me be perfectly candid with you, Kevin: your playing simply doesn't have that innate animal power. It is good, quite good. But it lacks a muscular skin—that effortless sense of phrasing and surface coherence—that distinguishes the truly great performers.

No, Kevin, your gift is for something else: a sense of form, an understanding of the mechanics by which a composer translates essence into sense. This is exactly the kind of understanding that should be communicated to students. In addition, you have a wry humor that would stand up well in the classroom. You have the poise to teach a class, and you have the values to lead it in the right direction.

I am not trying to make you a clone of myself. At my age, those things don't matter any more. But I want you to choose the right path. People do make wrong decisions, and those decisions can throw their whole lives out of kilter.

Great performers often lead lonely and eclipsed lives. They serve themselves and their instruments. But a teacher has a higher goal: he serves the music. Our frail human lives are given dignity by the common cultural heritage we share with other lives, past and future. That heritage—that and the children—are all we can pass on. I know you have the stuff within you to take up that great tradition and carry it forward. You're a fine young man, Kevin, and I'd hate to see you lose your better self in your frustration to be something that you aren't.

How is that beautiful young woman who thinks so much of you? Don't let her slip away. She's a jewel; take good care of her. Perhaps you know I lost Wilma this fall. Cancer. Enough said.

The music and the children are all that live on, Kevin. Please take what I've written to heart.

With affection,
Prof B.

Kevin threw down the letter, stood up, walked over to a window, and rested his forehead against the cold, dark glass. He stood there a few minutes, motionless; then, all of a sudden, he slammed his right hand against the wall. The hand throbbed and his knuckle was bleeding, but taking no heed of it, he returned to the music stand, took out his violin, and tried to practice. But he found he couldn't focus.

About ten the phone rang again; it was Suzanne.

"Russell has offered to go out and search for them," she said. "Do you want to go with him?" Her voice was full of suppressed emotion.

"Of course I'll go," Kevin said, welcoming the distraction.

"Get ready. He'll be by in a few minutes. Be sure to wear something warm."

"Okay."

Kevin put away his violin, bandaged his hand, and got out his oilers and boots. He found some comfort in putting them on: they symbolized his ability to get along in the world. No matter what, he could survive.

Russell pulled up and beeped a few minutes later, and Kevin walked outside to join him.

"How you doing?" Russell asked.

"Okay, I guess," Kevin replied. Russell didn't say anything else, but drove in silence to the boat.

Moonlight lay on the water like the rippling skin of an animal. As they made the long journey from town to Madaket, long, barrel-like waves surged forward with them. A rhythm soon established itself: the boat surfed for a while on one wave, slipped off to the side, then caught the next wave. Russell peered intently ahead, swinging the wheel quickly to bring the stern back each time it slipped to the side. If they were caught broadside by one of these waves, they could take in a lot of water, possibly go over. It wasn't likely, but it could happen. And with the water temperature 42 degrees, they wouldn't last long.

Russell had a can of beer nailed up under the forward deck, so that if he ever knew he wasn't going to make it, he could die happy. It was his last reward to himself for giving up drinking and settling down and getting married. He had vowed never to drink another beer—except for this one, when his time came. But all that was changed as of last night. He didn't know what it meant, exactly: whether he was slipping back into his old ways, or whether he was strong enough now to have a beer now and then, no sweat.

But one thing was clear: something funny was going on inside him. Maybe it had to do with the pressures of scalloping and building a house at the same time. Some days, late in the evening, it seemed like a part of his brain was pulling free of his control and thinking its own thoughts. Just last night, when Sam woke up crying in the middle of the night, he had an impulse to throw him down on the floor and tell him to be quiet. Such feelings frightened him in passing, but he was so busy that he hardly had time to think about them. He had a sense, though, that his emotional bond with Sam and Mary was slipping. Sam no longer seemed to expect as much from him; Mary seemed to be chiding him from a distance.

Looking out now on the moonlight and the waves, he felt that Sam and Mary were hardly real, that they had slipped away behind a bank of fog. He had to think that way to keep himself going eighteen hours a day; if he allowed himself the thought of Sam and Mary sleeping in bed, snuggled together under the covers, he would break down. That was how drained he was, how slender his resources were. His only recourse was to ignore them for the time being, and hope they would still be around when scalloping season finally ended.

They were nearing Tuckernuck. They came to the first of a series of several shoals. Russell pulled back on the throttle and brought the boat almost to a halt.

"Keep a sharp lookout on your side, Kevy," he said.

"Okay," Kevin replied. He peered over the edge. He

seemed more opaque tonight than usual: Russell had no idea at all what he was feeling. He imagined Kevin must be pretty upset, not knowing where his girlfriend was. If so, Kevin didn't show it. But then, that was true of most small guys, they never did.

Russell steered around one shoal and started toward another. He was aware of being just a little careless. As far as he knew, the tide was still coming up, and he had some room for error. He pushed the throttle forward a tad. And then, all of a sudden, the boat shuddered and came to a stop. Russell shut the motor off, swearing. The bottom of the boat was snagged.

"Jesus," he said.

"What can we do?" Kevin asked.

"Absolutely nothing," he said. "Damn."

"How are we going to get off?"

"Just wait. The tide's coming up. It'll float us off eventually." Russell banged his arms against his sides and jumped up and down a few times to keep warm. "How you doing, Kevy?" he asked.

"Fine," Kevin said.

"You worried?"

"Should I be?"

Russell took a cigarette out of his pocket, lit it, and inhaled. "With anyone but Frank, yes. With Frank, no. No way. I don't know of a better captain than Frank, and that's a fact."

"Then something happened to Frank: heart attack. Stroke."

"Naw, Frank's in good condition. His time hasn't come yet."

"What do you think happened, then?"

Russell laughed. "The same damn thing that happened to us. They're hung up on one of these goddam shoals, waiting for the tide to come up."

"So they'll get off about the same time we will? And they'll be gone before we even get there?"

"Naw. Have a little faith, Kevy. We'll know if they're leaving: we'll see 'em and hear 'em. They can't be far away."

"Within calling distance?"

Russell didn't answer. He drew himself up to his full height and shouted. "Frank! Frank!" His voice died away into the water sounds, without an echo. "Frank!" he yelled again. "Frank!" He was quiet a moment. "You hear anything?" he asked Kevin.

"No," Kevin said.

"I thought I heard something," Russell said.

"You didn't."

"You didn't hear someone?"

"Nope. Believe me, I have better than average hearing. I've had it tested."

"Not a little voice in the distance answering?"

"Nothing," Kevin said. "Water washing on the shore."

"Well, I believe you, Kevy. But I thought I heard your lady answering."

Kevin shook his head.

Russell peered over the side. The moonlight was so bright he could see the bottom—the scallop shells and pebbles on the sand. It seemed easier to see than it had been a few moments ago.

"Oh, no!" he exclaimed. "Damn!" He slammed his hand against the side.

"What's the matter?"

"I miscalculated. The water is already falling. Low tide was at four. That means high tide was about ten. And it's eleven thirty now. Already falling."

"Oh, no!"

"Oh, yes. We're stuck here for the night."

"Great."

"We got one beer between us, and no blankets. Wonderful!" Russell said. He let out a wild hoot of laughter.

"Well, I suppose the worst that could happen is that we'll freeze to death," Kevin said.

"No, the worst that could happen is that we'll almost freeze to death."

"Look at the bright side. We can always write up our experience and sell it to *Reader's Digest*. They're always looking for awesome survival stories." Kevin stamped his feet. Already his toes were cold.

"Sure. Throw in a shark or two. Good idea, Kevy." Russell swore to himself. He wasn't afraid of the cold, though he had been on the water at night enough to know how unpleasant it would be. What bothered him more was the possibility that he had injured the bottom of the boat. The fiberglass on the bottom was now four years old, and not as resistant as it once was. It was exactly what he didn't need, to injure the boat in November, at the start of the season. With his finances stretched to the limit from building the house, there was no way he could possibly buy another boat, even on credit.

But there was nothing he could do about that now. There was nothing to do but forget it all. He climbed over the culling board and crawled up into the tiny forward cabin. He found a hammer and banged at the wood for a few minutes.

"What are you doing?" Kevin asked.

Russell didn't answer. But a few minutes later he emerged with a beer.

"Want to share this with me?" he asked.

"Sure," Kevin said.

Russell pulled up the flip-top, and the can exploded with a compact, quick burst.

"It's cold," Russell said.

"Unavoidably," Kevin commented.

"Do the honors," Russell said, handing the can to Kevin. Kevin took a sip and passed it back to Russell.

"How is it?" Russell asked.

"Not bad."

"This beer has been sitting there for three years—since the day Mary and I tied the knot." Russell threw his head back and took another swig. He was so unaccustomed to alcohol now that even a tiny amount affected him. As the alcohol entered his bloodstream, he found his thinking growing mellower, and he thought of Mary and Sam with a warm, distant glow of affection.

"There's nothing like having a family," he told Kevin. "Nothing. I mean, I've been through a lot. Done it all. Drugs, sex, booze, sailing—you name it. But by God, there's nothing like a family. Nothing can compare with it." He passed the can to Kevin. "Haven't you ever thought of starting a family?" he asked.

"Some day," Kevin said. "You already asked me that."

"Don't wait too long," Russell advised him, taking back the beer. "I have a brother, he just turned thirty-five, and he's never been married. I don't think he could get married now even if he wanted to. You get past a certain point, you're not flexible enough any more to live with someone else."

"That's probably true," Kevin said. "But I've still got time." He wasn't used to alcohol, either, and the beer had gone to his head. The cold air accentuated its effect. "Yep, there's still time," he added.

"Nice girl you've got there. Sorry. Nice woman. Don't want to get the libbers mad at me."

108

"She is nice." As he spoke, Kevin realized that he had been ignoring Sheri of late, taking her for granted, as though she were a part of himself.

"I love Nantucket," Russell said. "It's so goddam clear and pure. So alive. The oceans. The moors. Hard to believe it's all because of a glacier."

"Glacial deposit?"

"Yep. A glacier dragged this whole island down from the north. Tuckernuck too. Tuckernuck got dropped off first, then in its dying gasp it let Nantucket go. Quite an accomplishment for a single little glacier, huh?"

Kevin looked out over the water.

"What do you want from life, Kevy?" The question might have seemed fatuous in another context, but it struck Kevin as natural and normal.

"Something to do with music," he replied. The alcohol and the cold air freed his thinking, made room for new thoughts to take shape; he didn't mention his concert aspirations, as he normally might have.

"You sound pretty serious about the violin. Four, five hours a day. You want to perform someday in Carnegie Hall or something?"

"Yes and no." Kevin cradled the can of beer in his hands.

"All the practicing you did, all those years? What else would it lead to?"

"There's a number of possibilities. Teaching, for one."

"You going to be a teacher?"

Kevin stopped. This had slipped out without his even knowing it. "I don't know," he said with a shrug. "It's hard to say."

"Nothing wrong with being a teacher," Russell said. "Get the summer off. One of my brothers is a teacher."

Kevin was silent. He was watching a black mass hurtling toward them through the dark air. As it came overhead, edged by silver moonlight, he saw that it was a V of birds—large, unidentified birds with powerful wings.

"Brutal," Kevin said. "What kind of bird?"

"Swans."

"I take it back. I guess a swan could hardly be called brutal."

"A swan is the meanest, nastiest son of a bitch you'll ever meet."

"Swans?" Kevin asked. "The bird you see in all the pretty Disney movies?"

"Swans," Russell confirmed. He took the can of beer from Kevin, finished it off, and wiped his mouth with the back of his hand. "I've seen 'em attack guys who were out in dories setting lines."

A shift in the wind brought back a symphony of creaking feathers, of rushing space.

"Where're they going this time of night?" Kevin asked.

"Who knows?" Russell said. "They probably don't know themselves." He leaned over and spat into the water. "Well, Kevy, we gotta get some sleep."

"Sleep?" Kevin asked. "Won't we freeze if we lie down?"

"Naw, we'll be okay. We'll go up forward under the cabin where our body heat will last longer."

Russell took a final swig and tossed the beer can into the water. The falling tide drew the can away from the boat.

"Farewell," Kevin intoned, with a solemn salute.

"I'll help it on its way," Russell said. He undid the straps to his oilers and unzipped the fly on his diving suit. Kevin did likewise on the other side of the boat.

"Maybe between the two of us we can raise the tide enough to float us off of here," Kevin said.

Russell laughed, listening to the water sounds. He zipped his fly back up and turned toward Kevin.

"For a serious guy, you can be pretty funny, Kevy," he said.

"We're funniest when we're most unhappy," Kevin said.

"You really believe that?"

"Yeah, I do." Kevin pulled his oilers up and turned toward the large dark figure on the other side of the boat. He shrugged. "That's how it seems to me, anyway."

"I know what you mean, Kevy. I know what you mean. Nothing else to do but laugh, right?"

"Right."

Russell beamed pleasantly at comprehending this idea. But then a new thought disturbed him. "What you unhappy about, Kevy?"

"I don't know," Kevin said. He had a sudden sense of speaking honestly and truly, with no pretense. His voice was simply part of the night. "I guess I have to decide what I'm going to do with my life."

"Nobody ever decides that. You just do what you have to, and you die."

"Sometimes you have to make choices."

Russell thought about this. "Maybe you're right. I've got ideas. Dreams," he said. "Big and little. Like building a house. That's the biggest dream. Little dreams too. One day, I want to have a big feast right out on the boat for lunch. White tablecloth, the works. Really get everybody's goat."

"But it isn't simply a question of dreams. There are choices—between dreams, if you will."

Russell thought a moment more, but now his mental energy was wearing thin. "Well, I'm ready to make a choice. I'm going to bed."

"Good idea. Sweet dreams."

Kevin followed Russell into the cabin. There was a narrow ledge along each side of the hull; those were their beds for the night. Russell lay on the port ledge, Kevin on the starboard. The tops of their heads were almost touching where the two ledges met at the bow.

"Not too bad, eh?" Russell said.

"Naw," Kevin said. He was already shivering. He brought his knees up to his chest.

"You must be worried about her."

"Yeah. I guess I am." But more than fearing that Sheri might be hurt or in peril on the sea, Kevin was disturbed by the sight of the swans. Somehow he associated the swans with Sheri, and he was disturbed to see them flying around like that, sailing wild and dark and silver across the face of the night.

He thought about Frank's wife, Suzanne, being alone in the night too, wondering; and then he thought about Mary and Sam, also alone.

"Say, Russell, thanks for offering to go out tonight looking for them."

"Aw, hey, Kevy. . . ."

"I'm sorry it turned out this way."

"Shoot, it's not your fault, is it? Now don't worry." Russell yawned and stirred slightly. "I just better not drink any more beer, or Mary will kill me."

"You gotta have some alcohol in your veins on a night like this. For antifreeze," Kevin said. Russell didn't respond. He was already asleep.

Kevin lay awake, shivering. He thought about how awful it would be to fall overboard at this time of year. He listened to the water noises; there seemed to be a pattern to them, as though someone were swimming around the boat and gently tapping it with a rubber hammer.

He still felt disturbed about Sheri, he didn't know why.

The arpeggiated section of Bach's Chaconne went through his mind—not as he played it but as it should sound, a taut formation of thrusting harmony. In his state of half sleep, the sound took on texture and dimension, became a structure with depth and height. He was climbing up its smooth surface but slipped and fell, and he lay on his back, admiring it as it rose into the clouds.

A ribbon of light wound through Kevin's mind. He was trying to wrap himself in it to escape the cold; then he realized it was morning and he could wake up. Russell was still asleep; his arm lay across Kevin. Kevin slipped out from under the arm and crawled out of the cabin. It was very early morning, no later than five thirty. Sheets of mist rolled over the water; the water undulated with clumsy, confused motions, like someone in restless sleep. The tide had lifted them off the shoal and moved them toward the shore. It must be Tuckernuck.

Now that it was daylight, it seemed to Kevin that Sheri was all right. In fact, she was probably somewhere close by. But he thought again of the swans and shivered. He had a funny feeling that he had lost her just when he was realizing how he needed her.

Russell emerged from the cabin, blinking his eyes and yawning. His huge face was pink and puffy, and his eyes were tiny slits.

"Well, we survived. I guess," he said, his voice thick and sleepy. He crossed his arms and banged his hands against his shoulders. "I'm still alive. Are you?"

"Too soon to tell. Is that Tuckernuck?" Kevin asked.

Russell's eyes opened wider as he looked.

"Yep," he said. "If you look close through the fog, you can see the weather vane on top of the house that belongs to Frank's sister."

"Should we go on looking for them?"

"Yep. With any luck, it won't be long now."

He climbed over the culling board into the stern and started up the engine. Slowly and cautiously, he inched the boat through the mist, at barely more than an idle. Kevin stood in the bow, peering ahead.

"Look!" he exclaimed.

Not far ahead, about a hundred yards from shore, a boat swung on its anchor line. It was a new, sleek Sea Ox, the kind of boat that made Russell both envious and doggedly proud of his own tank.

"That's Frank's boat, all right," Russell said. He sped up slightly until he reached the other boat. Then he cut the motor.

"Hey! Wake up!" he yelled. There was no answer. He bent over and looked inside. "They aren't here," he said.

"You think they spent the night on Tuckernuck?" Kevin asked.

"Very likely. Frank's no dummy. Why sleep out on a cold boat like we did, when you can be in a warm bed?"

Russell swung the boat around and brought it over toward shore. He stopped in about three feet of water and threw out an anchor.

"We'll have to walk in," he said. "I don't want to run the chance of getting stuck again. The tide shouldn't be falling again for a while, but you can never be sure around here. They don't just have a high and low tide here, you know. They have a west tide, an east tide, a high tide, a low tide, a back tide. The only guy who really understands them is Frank."

"If Frank knows, why did he get stuck?"

Russell shrugged. "It was probably a new shoal. They're forming all the time."

Kevin had the distinct impression, now that they were closer to finding Sheri and Frank, that Russell was deliberately making small talk.

They stepped into the shallows. Icy water poured over the tops of Kevin's boots, filling them to the ankles.

"Arhh!" he exclaimed. Russell made no comment.

Kevin slogged onto the shore; the water in his boots slowly grew warmer from contact with his feet. They crossed the beach and struck a narrow path leading up the hill. Patches of mist drifted around them. Silently, they climbed the hill and stopped by the cluster of houses.

"It's the one up there," Russell said. They went to the door and Russell peered in the window.

"Well, Kevy, I think our mission was successful. I see dishes in the drainer. Someone's been here." Russell was talking in an unusually loud voice, even for him, and again Kevin had that sense that Russell was making small talk.

"Is the door locked?"

Russell tried it. "Open," he proclaimed. "Let's take our boots off outside so we don't track in mud." He pulled off his boots and set them by the door. Kevin tried to slip off his boots, but they wouldn't come off; the water inside them created a strong suction. He sat down and yanked one off, and a stream of water poured onto him from the upturned boot. Russell was inside already. Faintly in the distance, Kevin heard voices. He struggled to pull off the other boot. Finally, it popped off. He slid into the kitchen on wet socks just as Russell was coming in from the other side.

"I found 'em," Russell said. He stood in the doorway between the kitchen and the hall. His eyes shifted about the room, avoiding Kevin. "Found Frank, that is. Sheri's in the bathroom."

"I'll go see her."

"Ah, I'd wait a minute if I were you, Kevy. Frank's just getting up, and, well, he's sort of a bear in the morning."

"What does that have to do with Sheri?"

Kevin pushed past Russell and strode down the hall. The door to the bathroom was open, and no one was inside. Just then, the bedroom door opened—and out came Frank, pulling the door shut behind him. His shirt was half buttoned and his blond hair was ruffled.

"Morning, gents," he said.

"Where's Sheri?" Kevin asked.

"I don't know. Still asleep, I guess," Frank said.

He shuffled down the hall, limping noticeably. Russell stood aside to let him by.

Kevin burst into the bedroom. Sheri was standing by the bed, half dressed. When she heard the door open she clutched a blanket and pulled it in front of her.

"Kevin!" she exclaimed. She still held the blanket tightly to her body.

"Are you okay?" he said. He went over and hugged her. But something was wrong. She was looking off over his shoulder, and she was limp in his arms, distant.

Kevin knew then, without asking, and turned away. Her hand lingered on his shoulder a moment, then slid off. In silence she finished dressing. Then she leaned down in front of the vanity, glanced at her face briefly, as though ashamed of this display of concern about her appearance, and shook back her long, dark hair.

"Ready?" she said. He motioned to her to go first, ahead of him.

When they came out into the kitchen, he knew by the conscious way Frank ignored her that his guess was correct. He walked outside, pulled his boots back on, and continued down toward the boat, without waiting to see if anyone was following.

"Kevin?" Sheri called out to him. "Don't you want some breakfast?"

Kevin didn't turn or answer. "I guess he's not hungry," Russell was telling the others. He imagined Russell shrugging, smiling, maybe giving a wink to Frank. He walked on. Sheri hadn't followed him. He came to the beach and sat down near the boats. In his mind he was hearing the arpeggiated section of the Chaconne again, and it seemed to him the one pure and beautiful thing in a tide-racked world.

It was a fine autumn morning. The fog had lifted and was drifting away, and patches of brilliant blue sky were appearing. The sun had climbed well over the horizon. Gulls cried hungrily; pipers ran along the sand in quick, timid bursts.

Behind him, the moon floated low in the west, pale as the vanishing mist. Kevin closed his eyes and felt the sun on his skin. A few minutes later there was a light touch on his shoulder. Sheri was beside him. She bent over and kissed him on the ear. He neither pulled away nor responded.

"Thank you for coming to look for me," she said. "You were stuck out there all night, my poor guy. You must have been so cold."

"I guess you found a way to avoid being cold," he couldn't help saying.

She didn't try to deny it.

"It was a fluke," she said.

"Is that the story you and he have come up with?"

"It's the truth."

"God, Sheri, he's old enough to be your father."

"That's beside the point."

There was no apology in her manner, and he didn't consider the possible effect of his self-absorption over the past few months. It seemed unimportant to share with her the thoughts set in motion by Professor Blatt's letter. They sat beside each other in silence, looking out over the water.

A few minutes later, the others came down the path. It was time to go back to Nantucket.

"Thank God it's Sunday," Russell was saying. "We couldn't go scalloping even if we wanted to."

CHAPTER 8

Suzanne had been up all night, and it was difficult to believe that it was now morning and time for other people to be awake: it still seemed as if wakefulness should belong to her alone. The dawn brought Suzanne no joy. It only made Frank's disappearance seem more final.

She had been alone most of the time. Heather had sat up with her for a while, after she came in from a date, but about two she fell asleep. Mike had been out with friends all night and still wasn't home. To pass the long hours, Suzanne had sat at the loom, working off and on. From time to time she drowsed off, for a few minutes at a time, and each time she awakened it seemed that some wound had opened a little deeper in her. Where was he?

At first it seemed to her that he must have had a heart attack. He shouldn't still be scalloping at his age, he was exhausting himself. She should have forced him to stop.

But the more she thought about it, the more certain she became that it wasn't a health problem. She would know, she would feel it, if he wasn't well—and she had no such feeling. But she had a horrible sense that something was wrong.

She tried to tell herself it was a minor problem with the boat, nothing more. One time a few years earlier, Frank had run out of gas and not come in on time. But even then he wasn't out all night. He had paddled in to shore, found a telephone, and called her to come get him. She rushed over, all concerned and worried, and when she picked him up he glanced at the seat beside her and said, "Where's my beer?"

"I didn't bring one, honey," she replied, caught off guard.

"What! I've been out all day and you didn't even bring me a beer?"

"Honey, I've been so worried about you. The last thing I would think of is a beer!"

"You remember the unimportant things, and you forget the important things, Suzanne."

She had to smile now, thinking of it. The funniest thing about it was, he had really meant it. Oh, it had partly been a way of preserving his dignity, but he had also really meant it. Because he didn't fear for his safety out on the sea, he couldn't imagine anyone else doing so either. That was just the way he was: the way of the Hussey family, seafarers for generations.

Suzanne had been born a Gardner—like the Husseys, one of the old families of Nantucket. She was several years younger than Frank but had known him by reputation at school. Frank was a hell-raiser but a good kid—the type teachers secretly like, despite the discipline problems they cause. When he was sixteen Frank quit school and joined the Merchant Marine. It was wartime then, and at eighteen Frank joined the Navy. Suzanne was sent to live with some relatives in western Massachusetts. After the war she attended the University of Massachusetts, developed a liking for the mainland and the mountains, and wasn't even sure she wanted to go back to Nantucket. But at the request of her family, she decided to try it—for a while. About that time, Frank came back too. He had decided to settle on the island and go scalloping and lobstering.

He saw her on the street one day and shouted hello.

"You Suzanne Gardner?" he asked, coming over to her.

"Yes," she replied. "You Frank Hussey?"

He was handsomer than she remembered. She liked the way he carried himself: he was lithe, sprightly, self-assured.

"Of course," he said. "Who else?"

"I don't know."

She turned away then. Something about his manner was just a little too presumptuous for her taste.

"Hey, where're you going?" he asked.

"What's it to you?"

"You want to have a soda with me?"

She glanced back at him archly.

"Come on!" he said. And before she knew it, he had her by the arm and was leading her over to Congdon's Pharmacy. She was convinced now that he was hopelessly conceited, and she dreaded the worst: a long windy series of sea stories, enlivened by immodest accounts of his exploits. But it didn't turn out that way. Once they were seated at the counter, he was suddenly shy. He didn't seem to know what to say; he might make an initial observation about something, but she had to keep the conversation going. She was relieved, if not especially impressed.

They started going out. It was spring, and the goldfinches and indigo buntings had come to the island, brilliant yellow and sky blue. Frank knew the names of all the birds, and he took obvious pleasure in sharing his knowledge with her. They spent long hours together rediscovering the island. They went for walks at dusk, as the moors faded from rose to gray. They found wild growths of lilac and wisteria and counted osprey nests. Suzanne enjoyed their time together; she was growing fond of him. But as time went on, Frank grew distant and uncommunicative. His mother was quite ill that spring, but he wouldn't talk about it. Sometimes Suzanne wasn't exactly sure why they were together, except that they both liked the moors.

When she first returned to Nantucket after her stay in western Massachusetts, the moors had struck her as flat and unattractive. But the more she saw of them, the more they haunted her. And the longer she stayed on Nantucket, the more subtle its appeal became: the close-knit community, the shared life-style, the familiar ways of the people, which she had always taken for granted but which she saw now in a new light. She was beginning to realize the quiet dignity of a small community trying to survive so far out at sea. She knew, if conditions were right, that she might be persuaded to stay.

But she would only stay for good reason, and while she hadn't defined in her own mind exactly what that meant, she knew she would recognize it if it came along.

That May Frank's mother died, and Frank asked her to come with him to the funeral. As the coffin was lowered, he was ashen and trembling, and he wouldn't talk.

About a week later, he rowed her out to Tuckernuck for a picnic. They spread their blanket on the moors near the Hussey house—which would soon belong to Frank's sister, as Frank was inheriting the family house in town. Suzanne talked cheerfully, trying to ease his mind, but he remained gloomy and withdrawn.

"When I die, I don't want to be buried," he said suddenly.

"What do you want?" she asked.

"I want my ashes to be spread at sea."

"That day is a long way off, Frank," she said, taking his arm.

He didn't speak for a long time. Then he looked over at her. "Suzanne, it isn't going to be easy to fill that big house in town. Will you help me?"

He had spoken in such a matter-of-fact way that she didn't know how to respond. She looked away, waiting for him to go on. He had never even told her he loved her.

But instead of going on, he stood up abruptly and walked away. He stopped about twenty feet off, with his back to her. His body was shaking.

She walked over to him, took his hand, and tried to get him to look at her. But he stubbornly turned away.

"Frank, I don't think this is the time to talk about it," she said. "Everything is still too . . . too recent and overwhelming for you."

He shook his head. He was like a small boy who won't speak, and she found herself growing angry.

"Frank, you haven't even told me what your feelings are for me."

He pulled away then and walked off. She sat down and waited, looking over the moors. She knew that the shape of her life hung in the balance—whether she would stay on Nantucket or whether she would leave—but she felt curiously at peace and unafraid.

The sun sank in the west; dark shadows filled the glacial valleys, bringing out the irregularities in the terrain. She knew then how much she loved this land, how much she loved these moors. But she could leave them, and she would, if it became necessary.

The shadows inched up to the tops of the hills. Behind her, Suzanne felt a presence. She turned. It was the full moon, hovering just over the horizon, still pale, almost translucent. She watched as it moved higher into the sky; she watched it gather all the light of the world unto itself. There was a sweep of feathers overhead; an owl was out hunting. A few stars showed. Then there was a rustling in the brush, and he was back.

"Suzanne?" he asked. His voice was resolute, willed to courage.

"Here," she said. He came closer and put his hands on her shoulders. His touch was rough but gentle.

Overhead, a V of Canada geese swept by, honking despondently.

"It's so awful in the spring," he said, "when someone is dying. It was so hard to watch it happen to her."

He began to cry, and she pressed her hands onto his. A southerly breeze stirred her hair, full of fragrance from the unfolding moors.

"I don't know what I would have done without you. I want to spend our lives together and start our own family. I don't want everyone to die." He was crying still.

She turned to him and put her arms around him. She kissed him on the lips, on the cheeks and forehead. She loved the smell of his skin. "There's living, too. We'll fill up that old house," she told him.

"Umm-huh," he said.

Suzanne went back to her work at the loom. She worked for about half an hour and then fell into another troubled slumber.

She didn't know how long she slept, but when she awoke the room was different. She felt the difference right away, though she didn't know what it came from.

Then she saw him, sitting at the table, his back to her. He was drinking a bottle of beer.

"Frank!" she exclaimed, getting up and going over to him. Her vision was misty; images passed before her eyes in waves.

He turned, and something in his eyes was confused and distant. But momentum carried her up to him, and she threw her arms around him and pressed her head against his neck. He smelled different, some new odor was on his skin. She knew right away.

"After all I go through," he was saying, "I come home and there ain't even a beer in the refrigerator for me. Had to go downstairs and find me a warm one."

She was laughing and crying, but underneath she knew his joking wasn't happy at all.

She pulled back from him, still holding his hands. "What happened, Frank?"

He lifted his arms and let them fall on the table. "I ran 'er aground," he said. "There's a new shoal out there, and boy did I hit her! My eyes failed me. Pretty sad thing to happen to an old man, eh?"

"But what did you do? Where did you sleep?"

"Walked in to shore to Betsy's house."

"Is Sheri all right?"

"Sheri? She's fine." The nonchalant tone confirmed her worst fears. She turned away from him, took some eggs and bacon out of the refrigerator, and set them on the counter by the stove, in front of the cooking sherry.

"Did Russell find you?" Suzanne asked, as the bacon began to sizzle. The sound helped numb her reactions, enclosing her in a private shocked world.

"Yeah, he found us," Frank said. "This morning. When it was too late to help."

Suzanne turned away. Tears were streaming down her face. She walked over to her loom and rested her hand on the smooth, polished wood. Looking across the room at her, Frank was unable to move or speak. She drifted out of the room and found herself sitting with her head in her hands at the dining room table.

Heather came into the room a few minutes later.

"What's wrong, Mom?" she asked, stopping a few feet away.

Suzanne nodded toward the kitchen. Heather looked in through the doorway.

"Oh, hi, Dad," she said in her nonchalant way. "Had a long night of it, huh?"

"Hi, honey," Frank said.

"Is something burning?" Heather asked.

"Sure smells like it, don't it."

Heather walked over to the stove and took the bacon and eggs off the heat.

"What's wrong with Mom?" she asked.

"I don't know," Frank said. "Maybe she hoped she was rid of me for good."

Suzanne took a deep breath and regained control of herself. She wiped her eyes and walked back into the kitchen. Taking the pan from Heather, she scraped the eggs and bacon onto a plate. Heather looked up at her and with characteristic directness asked, "You all right, Mom?"

"I'm fine," she said.

Heather looked back and forth between her parents. "I'm going cycling with Sally," she said. "See you later." She looked at them once more; there was a puzzled expression on her face as she turned to go.

Suzanne set the food in front of Frank. While Frank ate she busied herself cleaning the pan. It was an old, heavy iron skillet, coated with years of grease, and the burnt eggs came out easily. But Suzanne took a long time at the task, and when she was done she lifted all the burners off the stove and cleaned under them. She moved the spices and cookbooks and wiped off the counter beside the stove. She put the cooking sherry back in the cupboard where it belonged and closed the cupboard door securely. All this time she kept her back to Frank.

"Umm-huh," he said, getting up. He came over to Suzanne and rubbed her shoulders. "Nice to be back, hon," he said.

She wheeled toward him. Her look was so honest and clear that his surprised eyes didn't have the chance to look away or deny. She saw his golden eye register something; his gray eye as always seemed to remain neutral. He couldn't speak, and she found it unnecessary to do so. She picked up her keys and walked out the door.

Frank stared after her. He knew she knew, though he didn't know how. He hadn't had a chance to think through any of the recent events, and his feelings were all jumbled. He was still standing there when Mike came stumbling in. His eyes had that wild glare again, his pupils wide enough to drive a truck through. Frank felt a flush of sympathy for the kid, whose confusion up to this point had always struck him as something to be scorned.

"Good morning, Mike," he said.

"Morning," Mike answered, with the slight sneer that he reserved for his father. He walked on, not expecting any further interaction.

"Want some coffee?"

"No, thanks. Need a little sleep."

"Been up all night?"

Mike stopped and looked over toward his father, and something told him it was all right to be honest.

"Yeah, me and the guys had a pretty wild night."

Frank tried to respond in some way that would show he understood. But all he could say was, "Well, it happens sometimes."

Mike gave him a funny look and walked out of the room. Frank watched him go and then, feeling there was nothing else he could do, he went into the bedroom, lay down, and fell asleep.

Almost automatically, as she did every Sunday morning, Suzanne was driving to church. It was just after eleven; the service would still be in progress.

She slipped into the back with a sense of relief. But that sense quickly faded. Far from being lifted out of herself into a larger community of faith, she felt marked out, separate, apart from everything that was going on. Her favorite hymns felt meaningless on her lips. The people she most cared about seemed distant and foreign. She saw her brother and Frank's friend Milton up near the front but was not moved to join them. She felt like a sick child who has been told to stay in her room but creeps downstairs and peeks through the doorway at the dinner in progress, the merry conversation, the shared jokes, the spread of food—and finds because she is ill that they hold no attraction for her after all.

What was worse, as she looked around it became clear to her for the first time how much work the church really needed. Large sections of plaster were crumbling off the walls; the ceiling paint was cracking and peeling. She recalled hearing sometime in the past two days—since the meeting Thursday night—that the church had been found to be structurally unsound, that it would be condemned unless extensive renovations were done. These thoughts added to her gloom, as the minister's resonant baritone filled the church with his gentle, reasoned statements.

At first Suzanne hardly listened to his words, but her attention was caught momentarily when she realized his subject matter. He was discussing "The Mat-Maker," a chapter from *Moby Dick*. It was the only part of that long book that Suzanne knew at all well; a portion of the chapter was framed and hung next to her loom.

The passage discussed necessity, free will, and chance in terms of a loom. Necessity and free will were interwoven like warp and woof; chance stamped them into peculiar configurations. Using this text as his starting point, the minister was discussing whether an individual can be held responsible for his actions, if indeed he is not totally free to decide them. Suzanne followed his argument for a few minutes: apparently he believed the individual had to be held responsible. Her mind drifted, and she lost his line of reasoning. But she filed away the issue for future consideration.

Suzanne's arrival had gone unnoticed except by one person, Maude Miller. Maude sat in the back every Sunday, so as not to distract the rest of the congregation when she left to go to the ladies' room.

She saw Suzanne come in, and when Suzanne tried to slip away after the service, she stopped her.

"Will you pay a visit to a lonely old lady?" she asked in her low, throaty voice.

"I'd love to," Suzanne said, with the courtesy habitual to her. As she spoke, Suzanne remembered that Maude was Sheri's great-aunt. The realization struck her numbly.

"Meet me at my house in ten minutes," Maude said, waving her hand at Suzanne to go out before the others caught her.

Ten minutes later, Suzanne joined Maude in her living room, which was furnished with old, worn Victorian furniture. After tea was served, Maude sent her live-in nurse out of the room and went right to the point.

"Now, my dear, tell me what's making you so unhappy," she said.

"I . . . why do you ask?"

Maude shook a finger at Suzanne. "You're not yourself this morning. I could see it as soon as you came in."

Suzanne was silent a minute. "Frank slept with another woman last night," she said finally, curious as to how she would feel as she pronounced those words.

Maude looked at Suzanne with dull, unblinking eyes. A peculiar, tender smell like damp wool seemed to come from her body.

"Worse things have happened," she said. She thought a moment. "May I ask one awfully personal question? Was it a mutual friend?" She watched Suzanne carefully as she spoke.

"No," Suzanne replied, looking down.

Maude's eyes glittered almost imperceptibly. Suzanne knew she knew who it was; Suzanne also knew that Maude, out of delicacy, would not mention it.

"It's better that it wasn't a friend. Still, it's a disappointment," Maude said. "It is a disappointment. Did he tell you?"

"No."

"I don't like that," Maude said. She took out a cigarette, placed it between her lips, and struck a match. She inhaled deeply, shook the match, and put it down. Smoke poured out of her nostrils. "They tell me these things are killing me. But I say, why stop now? The damage is done, and I'll be damned if I'm going to give them up at this late date."

She smoked in silence for a minute, looking at the ceiling.

"Well, he'll give her up, but will *you* give it up?" she asked.

"I'm afraid I don't understand," Suzanne said.

"Yes, you do." Maude leaned forward and tipped the ashes onto her saucer.

"I don't know that he will give her up. I don't know what's going on."

"They always give them up. Of course, it would help if you made your feelings known—something I'm not sure you're very good at. You need to learn to assert yourself, be a little more stubborn, like Maude the mule, who's already been around too long but is too stubborn to die."

"You haven't been around that long," Suzanne said, smiling in a way that made her seem girlish.

"Long enough," Maude said. "I don't have much longer." She picked up the package of cigarettes and rattled it. "These will see to that."

"You may surprise yourself."

Maude laughed; her laughter lost itself in a volley of coughing.

"No, dear," she said, when she could speak again. "You know, I've always thought it's as simple as the ferryboat: you get on, you have your ride, you get off. I've had my ride, and soon I'll be getting off."

Suzanne looked into Maude's eyes and saw that she was speaking without self-pity. "Would that I had your strength," she said.

"Strength!" Maude said, with a wave of her hand. "It's not as if I have any choice in the matter." She smoked another minute in silence.

Suzanne felt it was time for her to leave. But when she stirred, Maude gestured to her to be quiet.

"What's the most beautiful thing you've ever seen?" she asked.

Taken by surprise, Suzanne said, "I don't know—dawn over Tuckernuck, I guess." Then she felt the new resonance that Tuckernuck had for her, and she shivered inwardly. She didn't go on to paint the image she had of Tuckernuck's dawn—the cormorants, the pale patina of colors, the unbroken moorlands falling into the distance. . . .

"You're wrong, you know," Maude told her.

"I beg your pardon?"

"You're wrong. You've missed the whole point."

"What point?"

"This: the most beautiful thing, out of this whole world, is a sleeping baby. The rest is all just . . . illusion."

Suzanne was silent a moment. "I don't know," she said.

"Sometimes, when I get discouraged, I try and remember that. Maybe it will help you."

"I'll think about it."

"You know, I think this even though I lost my own little girl. It's just . . . it's just the way things are. But you'd better go now; I can feel myself tiring." Maude shook her head and seemed to withdraw back into herself.

Suzanne took her hand. Maude nodded goodbye with averted eyes.

Suzanne walked outside to her car. She didn't know where she was going; she simply found herself driving. She drove out Vesper Lane, past the old graveyard. Her parents, her grandparents, and her great-grandparents were all buried there, Gardners all. Frank had married her and (as Sammy always told her) made a Hussey of her.

She came to Hummock Pond Road and followed it toward the shore. The pond lay on the right, a ribbon of silver light. For a moment, Suzanne remembered the pond as it was when she was a girl, surrounded by great fields of wild roses. It seemed to her now that she had spent her childhood wandering through the roses, drunk with the fresh, pungent fragrance. There were no houses then, just the wild, unbroken expanse of moors, the white arc of beach, and the great blue ocean.

No one had any idea that vacation houses would one day encircle the pond; no one ever had any idea that the island would be developed like this, its pristine appeal become such big business. But it had happened, and few of the natives had tried to stop it. Most of them had been seduced by the money of rich outsiders; they had allowed outsiders to move in and carve up the island for their own use. They had become bedfellows with strangers, off-islanders, all for a momentary pleasure that would alter the island forever.

It was difficult not to feel anger with the outside world and disappointment with Nantucket. Betrayals were going on daily, betrayals of all kinds.

Trying not to see them, Suzanne drove past the vacation houses and came to Cisco Beach. She parked the car and got out and walked out onto the sand, which stretched off in a curve toward the flat, unbroken horizon.

Several hours later, Suzanne still didn't feel like going home. She was about a mile down the beach from the car, sitting with her legs bent and her arms wrapped around her knees. The long sloped shoreline curved off into the distance, pale bronze in the clear autumn light. Waves raced in toward shore, teams of horses with flying manes. Behind her, the sand rose to a cliff, some twenty feet in height, at the top of which were rosa rugosa and bayberry. Suzanne could smell the delicate odor of the roses, and could make out the tiny gray clusters of bayberries.

When her children were little, Suzanne had sometimes brought them here to pick bayberries. They would take the berries home and boil them in water; the wax rose to the top, along with leaves and twigs and bugs. They would separate out the wax and use it to make tiny candles for Christmas. The whole house would smell of bayberry, an odor like peppermint and thyme compounded and intensified. The scent meant home to her; it meant small, happy children; it meant being happily married.

The strange thing was, the more she thought about what Frank had done, the more she wondered if it was really so bad. As Maude pointed out, worse things have happened. What did it matter, the sheer physical act? How did it even affect her? What did it matter, what he felt for Sheri? And when it came right down to it, which was worse: that he should care or not care for the girl? If he really cared for her, it made him more human in a way. But it was easier for her if he didn't care, if it was all just a freak; then she could brush it aside more easily. She hoped that was all it was, even if it diminished Frank in a way, even if it diminished her in a way too.

And the strangest thing was, she felt guilty about the whole thing, as though she herself had brought it on. Had she been loving enough to Frank? Had she begun to bore him? But as she found herself trying to shift the blame to herself, she only grew angrier with him.

Whichever way her mind ran, it kept turning back on itself. And the only thing she was left with was the image of Frank in bed with the girl, making love to her as though he had never made love to anyone else in his life. And no matter how Suzanne thought about it, that image carried as much hurt as anything she had ever experienced.

Had there been others? How many? Where? Had something always been wrong between them?

She thought and thought until there was nothing left to think; there was only the sea and the sky, merging at some line on the horizon that she couldn't distinguish. There was only the sea and the sky, a moving plane and a still dome, time and space, darkening. Her mind had room for no more thoughts. She could feel no more pain.

A white gull took flight against the darkness; her eyes lingered on it with all her love.

Sheri was painting in the small room at the back of the house that she had made her studio. Sunlight streamed in around her through the double glass doors, striking the dust motes that rose and fell in a wavelike motion around her. But she was hardly aware of her surroundings. She was engrossed in her picture, a portrait of a loaded culling board. The idea, which had originally struck her as humorous, now seemed totally serious, a subject worthy of the highest effort.

Scallops, with their familiar, radiated shell, filled most of the picture. She was including the widest range of scallops possible: from the small muddy ones in town to the giants at the Horseshed, from young seeds to old duds, from brown to black to yellow to orange. She had seen all of them, though never all at once in the same tow; but she felt it was valid to draw on the range of her experience and include everything in one canvas. Mixed in with the scallops were swaths of eelgrass, an old green bottle, a rusted iron spike, a flounder, a toadfish, a starfish, and, around the edges, a suggestion of sand and mud. She had seen all these on the culling board, too.

She wanted the painting to have a photographic clarity, but with a richness no photograph could convey. She wanted the painting to give a sense of the prodigality of the sea, but also of the sheer labor required to bring its creations to the table. To develop this last point, a human hand was half buried in a mound of eelgrass, and a flounder was wriggling away from the hand. The hand was rough, from years of work on the water, but it should look capable, even beautiful in its way. It was a hand that knew its place in the universe. Sheri was working on the hand today, with a mute, intent air. She was all alone; Kevin had blown up at her when they got home and had stalked out in a fit. But preserving her own inner equilibrium, she had come into this room and started right to work.

She lavished attention on the details of the hand: the forward thrust of the fingers as they disappeared into the grass, the arch of the palm, the straining of the muscle tendons. The hand was deep brown, with a fine criss-cross of wrinkles like the lines left on the sand by the receding tide. In fact, if the picture were to succeed, the hand would have to appear as much a creation of the seas as the scallops and eelgrass; the hand would have to appear as natural and inevitable as the other elements of the picture.

As she worked, it slowly dawned on her that there was a problem. The accumulation of detail took her farther and farther from what she wanted, and the hand, it was turning out, did seem out of place. Not because it looked too familiar and land-bound in the midst of the sea creatures; the problem was the opposite: out of all these strange and fanciful creations of the sea, the hand was the strangest and most foreign of all. The other elements—the scallops, the eelgrass, the starfish—rested on the canvas with innocent self-absorption; the hand practically leaped out of the picture by contrast. It looked as if it would swallow up everything else in the picture. It wanted to grasp and use and take everything and leave behind nothing but waste. It was all knuckle and sinew and rough-knobbed efficiency; it had none of the sea-worn, sea-softened appearance of the sea creatures. It was too young for the picture, too new, like a housing development in the midst of the moors.

Sheri put down the brush and sat on the floor with her head resting on her bent knees. She felt a revulsion with herself. She was like that hand, that reaching, clutching, too-young thing on the canvas. Oh, she had had a willing accomplice, but maybe he had less choice than it seemed. She had known implicitly the power of the young over the old, the gravitational pull of old to young. Hadn't she partly been testing that power, trying its limits? Wasn't it also partly a way of getting back at Suzanne for her older calm and inaccessible goodness? But mostly, it was the thrill of moving the old to obedience, of taming the thrust of the swan, as the moon draws the water across the face of the earth. The hand in the picture was not Frank's; it was her own.

Sheri knew, Frank knew, Kevin knew, Russell knew, and Suzanne knew. Suzanne told Maude and Russell told Mary, who told no one. None of the others told anyone. But by the end of the day, it was common knowledge on Nantucket that Frank and his culler had slept together, that Suzanne was beside herself, and that all was in disarray. It was impossible to say how news like this traveled so quickly in a small town; it was almost as though there were a network of nerves on the island, through which ideas spread at the speed of light, without the use of words. Perhaps from the accumulated hints and signs—which no one person had seen in their entirety, but which reassembled en masse were conclusive—it was evident to the general mind that Frank was dazed, Suzanne was unhappy, Sheri was brooding, Kevin was outraged, and Russell was sardonic; therefore, only one conclusion was possible. On the other hand, it may have been that the general mind sought to believe whatever was most titillating and required little food to stimulate the juices of its imagination. It is possible, given the externals of a grounding on a remote island and a man and a woman forced to spend the night together in close quarters, that the union would have been inferred even if nothing of the sort had happened: if Frank had slept out the night in the armchair, if Sheri had gone outside for another look at the moon and then gone to bed. It was even conceivable that Frank, waking to see the naked girl beside him, might have sworn a round oath at her and told her to get herself to bed before she caught her death of cold. That might have been his reaction five years earlier or five years later. But such was not the case, and the general opinion of the town about what happened was borne out by the events of the next few days.

CHAPTER 9

Russell didn't get home until about ten Sunday morning. After he hung up his oilers, Mary welcomed him with with a big hug and held up Sam for him to kiss.

"Thank goodness you're home," she said. "Is everyone all right?"

"Yeah, everyone's all right." Something in his tone wasn't convincing.

"Are you sure?" she asked.

"Oh, yeah." He rubbed noses with Sam. "Happy birthday, big guy," he said. Sam laughed and grabbed his dad's nose.

Russell took off his diving suit and went into the bedroom for pants and a shirt. When he returned, Mary said, "Okay, Russell, what is it?"

He put a kettle on the stove and turned to her. "Well, I don't know if I'm imagining it, but it sure looked like something is going on between those two."

"Who?"

"They were in bed together this morning when Kevin and I finally tracked 'em down."

"Frank and Sheri?"

"Yep."

Russell related the events of the night and morning, as Mary listened in silence. When he was finished she sat rigidly still, looking out the window.

"I'm going over to the house," Russell said.

"Don't leave now."

"I'm not tired," he said. "I slept better last night than I have in a year. Kevin doesn't cry at night the way Sam does."

"I want you to stay with me."

Russell raised his arms and lowered them in a gesture of frustration, but he took a seat beside Mary on the sofa. She leaned her head onto his shoulder and closed her eyes. Sam had fallen asleep on her lap for his morning nap.

"I feel so terrible for Suzanne," she said.

He grunted by way of reply, but she knew he wasn't with her; mentally, he was already over at the house, putting up wallboard. Her hand tightened on his arm.

"I'm worried, Russell," she said.

"Worried?"

"I feel like something terrible is going to happen."

"Nothing terrible's going to happen."

She raised her head and looked at him. "Russell, are you going to come back to us?"

"What?"

"Are you going to be able to return to normal when scalloping is over? Or are you going to slip farther and farther away, somewhere where I'll never see you again?"

He laughed uncertainly. "I don't know what you're talking about. I haven't gone anywhere."

She looked at him with her sad gray eyes. "Sam and I love you," she said.

"And I love you." He stirred in his seat; she knew he had to go.

"All right," she said.

He walked over to the door and turned. "You gotta come by later. There's gonna be a surprise."

After he was gone, Mary began to worry about Suzanne. She picked up the phone to call her but set it back down again. She didn't know what to say; she felt awkward and meddlesome. She appreciated more than ever the grace and tact with which Suzanne was able to help people.

But when it came to receiving help from others, Suzanne might have trouble. Mary suspected she wouldn't know how to accept it; she would push everyone away, politely but firmly, and let the hurt fester inside her.

She had to try, in whatever awkward, self-conscious way she could. And so, when Sam woke up from his nap, she dressed him in his sailor suit and drove over to Suzanne's house.

Normally the sight of the house comforted Mary, but today it seemed lonely and stricken, despite the roses that still bloomed on the trellis in front of the house. Suzanne's blue Rabbit wasn't in the drive. Mary slowed down momentarily and started to drive on. But she remembered that one of the children could have taken the car; she parked and carried Sam to the front door and knocked.

There was a confused banging inside, the sound of footsteps advancing and retreating, then silence. Just as Mary was about to leave, there were more footsteps—heavier, faster—and the door opened. It was Mike. His eyes regarded her distantly from behind his long lashes.

"Hi, Mike," Mary said. "Your mom home?"

"Dunno," he said. He yawned. "Wanna come in?"

"All right."

Mike turned and shouted, in a voice so loud that

Sam began to cry, "Hey, Mom, someone here to see you."

Mary followed Mike into the kitchen. Frank was sitting there, working on a scallop dredge.

"Hi, Frank," Mary said. She felt blood coming to her face at the sight of him.

"I guess Suzanne went out for a while," Frank said.

He looked shrunken and defiant and unaffected all at once as he bent over the dredge.

"You don't know where she went?" Mary asked.

"Usually on Sundays she goes to church. But she's been out awhile. She must have gone shopping afterward."

"Okay."

Frank made no effort toward further conversation. Sam walked up to him and tried to touch the dredge, but Frank waved him brusquely away. Sam took a step back; his lower lip quivered.

"Well, I guess we'll see you tonight," Mary said.

"Tonight?" Frank looked up.

"At Sam's p-a-r-t-y," Mary spelled out.

"His what?"

"He's one year old today."

"Oh. Congratulations," Frank said, with no special feeling. Mary turned and left. Her face was burning again. She put Sam in his car seat and found herself driving on the road to Cisco Beach.

There was no real reason to think she would find Suzanne at Cisco Beach, except that she dated the beginning of her friendship with Suzanne from a chance meeting they once had there. It came at a crucial point in Mary's life, when she and Russell were beginning to get serious about each other. Russell was still drinking heavily then, and one night he got drunk and simply went berserk. He threw things, he swore at Mary, he

142

made absurd, crazy boasts about himself. Finally, just before dawn, he passed out. Mary left him then and—not wanting to go back to her apartment—she drove out to Cisco Beach to watch the dawn. Just after sunset, a solitary figure walked down the beach toward Mary. It was Suzanne; it turned out that she often came to Cisco in the early morning. Sometimes, she could see Frank's sea-scalloping boat, which stayed out for a week or two at a time in the area south of Cisco.

Suzanne stopped and asked Mary if she was all right. Though she hardly knew Suzanne then, Mary spilled out her troubles. She felt a growing sense of well-being; she told Suzanne everything. Suzanne remained silent a few minutes and then voiced her opinion. It sounded to her that Russell was of two minds: he wanted commitment, but he was afraid of it. Some very good men were like that, and it made them behave strangely before big decisions like marriage. But Mary should have faith in Russell; he would come through. Suzanne knew him because he had worked for Frank, and she knew Frank thought highly of him. Mary should go back to him.

Mary returned to Russell's apartment just as he was waking up. His expression was childlike and open; he had a chastened, subdued air. They began to talk. He told her about his father, who had also had a drinking problem: finally his mother had told him to choose between her and alcohol. He chose alcohol. Russell was afraid he would do the same himself.

"Then stop," Mary said. "Just don't drink any more."

"I don't know if I can."

They made a pact that he would call her, any time night or day that he felt an urge to drink. The pact worked, and six months later they were married. Except for Suzanne, it might never have come to pass.

And so, three years later, Mary drove out to Cisco Beach in search of Suzanne. In the back of the car, Sam was fussing. Mary was sure he knew she was unhappy. He was a very sensitive boy. Like herself, Mary thought in passing. Or was he actually more like Russell, responding with inarticulate pain to things he didn't consciously recognize as painful?

She drove past Hummock Pond, past the litter of vacation houses, and came to the small beach parking lot. Just one car was there: Suzanne's small blue Rabbit.

Mary carried Sam down to the beach, which curved off in a long crescent. Lines of silver-blue waves swept in toward the pale blond shore. The shoreline was empty except for one small black dot in the distance. Mary hoisted Sam higher onto her hip and headed for that dot.

As she came closer to Suzanne, she had no idea what she would say; her mind was swept clean, as empty as the sand and water and sky. She didn't even know what was driving her forward: love, concern, the need to prove herself, perhaps even a morbid curiosity. She had momentary doubts about her motives, but it was too late.

Suzanne had not seen them coming and didn't look up until they were only twenty yards away. Her expression was totally unguarded; there was a listless, defeated look in her eyes that Mary had never seen there before. Mary ran the last few yards; dropping to the sand beside Suzanne, she reached out and hugged her. Sandwiched between them, Sam began to giggle and wave his arms and feet. Suzanne's shoulder blades felt so birdlike and frail, it made Mary want to hold her tighter and protect her. But Suzanne returned the hug only long enough to be polite and then pulled away.

144

"There, Sam," she said, "it wouldn't do for us to crush you now, would it?"

Mary knew then that Suzanne wouldn't talk. And trying to emulate Suzanne's tact, she decided to let Suzanne bring up the subject herself.

"Sam and I were going for a little walk," she said, "and we saw a dot down the beach, and look who it turned out to be, Sambo!"

Sam laughed and reached toward Suzanne, who picked him up and turned him around and set him in her lap. Then she bent forward and kissed him on his wide, low forehead.

"You have a big evening ahead, Sam," she said. "Does your mommy have everything ready?"

"Just about," Mary answered. "While I was staying up last night waiting for Russell, I went ahead and made the cake." Then, feeling she shouldn't have alluded to the past night's events, she quickly added, "So I'm way ahead."

Suzanne was looking out over the water. "It seems only yesterday that my children were little," she said.

"I still can't picture Sam being grown up," Mary said. She talked on in the happy, speculative tone she often used around Suzanne. "Will he really go out and work in the world? I just can't picture it."

"When you have the other one, that's when he'll seem old," Suzanne told her.

"What was it that Heather said about Mike when he was born?"

Suzanne smiled slightly, in appreciation. "Someone came up and asked Heather if Mike was her new baby brother," she recited. "And she replied, 'Oh, no, that's our home dwarf.'"

"Didn't that happen here, on Cisco Beach?"

Suzanne smiled again. "I didn't know you remembered everything I told you, Mary. Yes, it was right here, about a hundred yards down the beach."

Sam reached around and squeezed Suzanne's nose.

"Do they ever stop squeezing noses?" Mary asked.

"Not until they're ready to leave home and start their own families," Suzanne said with the tiniest suggestion of a wink.

"I think that will be wonderful. Being a grandmother, I mean. You have a lot to look forward to." Suzanne listened in silence as Mary bubbled on. "It's so wonderful how the center keeps changing, how each generation gets its turn. You know you'll be a grandfather one day, Sambo?" Mary pulled Sam back onto her lap and gave him a hug.

Suzanne was looking out over the water. "Not everything is pleasant about approaching the exalted state of grandmotherhood," she said, with a bitter edge to her voice which Mary had never heard before.

Mary felt the blood coming to her face. "Everyone loves you so much, Suzanne. You've helped us all in so many ways. And we . . . we just want to help you in any way we can."

Suzanne greeted the remark with a sardonic, sad smile. "I'm afraid there's no helping age, is there?" she said. Then she whispered something to Sam and played pattycake with him. Mary sat by, watching in helpless silence. A few minutes later Suzanne said she should be getting home. Mary walked back with her along the beach, utterly miserable. Sam was getting restless; he tried to squirm away, when Mary bent to put him in the car seat, and bumped his head on the door. He began to wail, and by the time Mary had calmed him down, she was in tears too.

Suzanne got into her car and backed it around. She stopped by Mary, rolled down her window, and said,

146

"Thank you for coming, Mary. It was really sweet of you." But something in her voice was disconnected from the words, and her smile had the same sardonic distance.

After leaving the beach, Mary swung by the apartment to pick up the decorations for the party. Russell had convinced her to have the party in the new house, though it was still unfinished inside: the walls were plasterboard with no skim coat or trim, and the floor was still just plywood. So Mary had bought a lot of balloons for decoration. Picking up everything for the party—the balloons and the snack food and the cake and presents—she drove out to the house. She carried Sam and a bag of decorations into the kitchen. The room had a chunky, overblown look; it reminded her for some reason of those cars with extra-large tires. But it was definitely becoming a room. She saw for the first time, with more than a theoretical knowledge, where the cabinets would go, where the sink would be. If she weren't still miserable from her meeting with Suzanne, she would have felt a rush of excitement.

"Hi, Russell," she called. "We're here."

She walked into the living room and stopped, stunned. She was greeted by perfectly smooth, white walls. Russell was standing there, grinning at her. His face was white with plaster and dust.

"Russell!" she exclaimed. "I don't believe it!"

She ran up to him, set Sam down on the floor, and gave him a hug.

"It's beautiful!" She had never believed that any part of their house would really be finished. She was so excited she didn't even stop to think about the smell of beer on his breath. "How did you do it?"

"I got a little help from Roger," he said. "This morning. He used to be a plasterer, you know."

Mary put her hand to her mouth and walked slowly around, in a circle.

"How am I going to put up the balloons?" she asked. "I can't make holes in the walls."

Russell shook his head, still grinning. He held a beer in his left hand. Sam came over to him and tugged at his pants.

"Hi, Sambo," Russell said. He moved a few steps away from Sam and took a sip of beer. Sam tottered after him and grabbed his leg again, laughing. Without looking down at Sam, or giving apparent thought to what he was doing, Russell pulled away again. He walked over to a window, set down the beer, measured for a piece of trim, and cut a pine board to length. Sam lost his balance, fell, and began to cry. Russell carried the trim over to the window, fished in his apron for some finish nails, and nailed the board in place.

Mary picked up Sam and stood watching Russell. He seemed propelled forward by some external force; he was totally oblivious of her and Sam.

Sam was crying again, out of boredom this time. Mary blew up a balloon and gave it to him to play with while she put up the decorations. She found some transparent tape in her purse and taped balloons to the walls. She strung up a few streamers.

She paused one last time for a look, and it suddenly became clear to her what had happened to Russell. He had been overwhelmed by the translation of dreams into reality. The house had begun for them as a dream of some unimaginable happiness in the future. Then, with stark realism, it had become a hole in the ground, a huge, empty hole. Later, when the foundation was finally built, the house (what there was of it so far)

148

looked very small—a few meager walls of cinderblock in the middle of a desert of sand and clay. But a few months later, when the deck and the outside walls were framed, it looked large again. And when the roof went up, it looked larger still. But then, after the interior walls were constructed and the wallboard put up, it looked small again. It looked small for a long time, as the slow interior work progressed. But finally, now that this room had been plastered and trimmed out, it once again looked large—as large as her original dream of the future. But her dream had never included how long it would take to get to the future—over a year—or how much waiting and work it would all be. Her dream had never included all the ups and downs, all the expansions and contractions, all the doubts along the way about the design, the placement of rooms, the details of doors and windows. Her dream had never included all the unpaid bills for lumber and electricians and plumbers.

But the main thing her dream had missed was the pressure. It was as though she and Russell and Sam had been living in a tiny room the past year, a room whose walls were closing in on them a few inches more each day. Gradually, over the course of the year, they had given up walking about, then standing, then moving their arms—until all they could do was to sit close together, arms and legs crossed, completely motionless. And the thing of it was, it had happened so gradually that it became the normal way to be. And now that a part of the house was finished, she had forgotten how to move about and enjoy it. Even with a finished house, she couldn't help but imagine that they would spend the rest of their lives huddled miserably together, like survivors of the arctic winter whose coats are so thick they can't feel the approach of spring.

*   *   *

Mary had known Russell wouldn't take the time to come home and change, that he would want to work on the house up to the last minute. So she didn't make an issue of it but instead made sure to bring a change of clothes for him. True to form, Russell insisted on working right up until seven. When the first guests knocked at the door, Mary ordered him into a back room to change. He emerged a few minutes later in his freshly pressed clothes, with sawdust and plaster dust still sprinkled over his face and beard.

The last time Mary had seen Russell in those clothes was for the dinner at Sheri's house, and by association she remembered that she had invited Sheri and Kevin to the party. Would they still come? Would Suzanne come? Would Frank come? Mary began to greet the guests.

Milton was the first to arrive. He stood in the middle of the room, looking around slowly, repeating, "Holy smoke, Russell, holy smoke," in his soda-bottle voice. "Jeez, you're really coming along." Russell stood there sipping at a beer and nodding his head, more in time with his own thoughts than in appreciation of what Milton was saying.

The rest of the barbershop quartet arrived in quick order. Jack came with his wife, Betty, and eyed the progress in the house with grudging, sarcastic pleasure. Suzanne's brother Sammy strolled in, with that look in his eyes as though he had known it would all come to pass and he didn't care much either way. With him was a woman, perhaps ten years younger than he, who had just been through a rather public divorce. Then, without any fanfare, Frank slipped in quickly through the door alone and went up to Milton. The quartet was now complete, and they went off into one of the back rooms to warm up.

A number of other guests also came, among them Roger, who entered the room with his characteristic jerky gait, his beard wagging and his eyes darting about. He stopped by Russell, who slapped him on the back but didn't say anything, and an expression of pride came into Roger's eyes

Mary looked around nervously. It was eight o'clock. Suzanne and Kevin and Sheri had still not shown up.

CHAPTER 10

That morning, when Kevin and Sheri got home from Tuckernuck, Kevin left the house again immediately, taking his violin case with him. He stopped just once, at a toy store, where he bought a birthday present for Sam. Then he turned down Madaket road and just kept walking. Before long he was surrounded on either side by open moors, which rolled off around him like a series of miniature gray mountain ranges. Without conscious thought, he turned off the road and made his way through the moors toward a hilltop. From there he could see Madaket harbor gleaming in the sun like a sheet of finely pounded metal. Gulls winged by overhead, making their way toward the nearby dump.

He sat down, half expecting something to become clear, some resolution to be reached. But nothing had changed. His thinking was as confused and aimless as it had been all morning. He still felt the same dull anger and sense of being wronged by Sheri. Yet at the same time, he knew it was more complicated than that.

Kevin was unsure of everything. Was Professor Blatt right about giving up his concert aspirations? At the time he read the letter (it was only yesterday, but it seemed weeks ago), it had opened only a small crack of doubt in his mind. But the events on Tuckernuck had pried open that crack, and he sensed the vague presence of an abyss below. There was something inviting about that abyss, about letting go and plunging through space.

The more he thought about the letter, the more it seemed undeniable. He had known it all along without wanting to face it. His drive to be a concert artist had been drawing more and more energy unto itself, growing too large for him to bear. It was inevitable that he should finally arrive face-to-face with his limitations. Normally, he would have resented having his limitations pointed out, but he had little energy left now for defiance.

He just had enough energy to take out his violin and try a final test. He tuned and launched into the fast section of the Chaconne, trying to listen with the detached ear of a critic. The notes sailed across the moors as taut as kite lines. A shadow fell across the sun; the birds grew quieter; he had the sense that the whole world was listening. His initial reaction was favorable. His playing *was* good: it did have that "muscular skin" the professor had referred to. But this was only his initial reaction, as he summoned all his remaining energy in a final burst of defiance. He managed to convince himself for about five minutes. Then he felt suddenly repulsed by his playing, and he stopped. The notes fluttered to the ground around him like confetti; they rained down around him on the moors with sad abandon. And the wind sent them scurrying away.

He put the violin away and sat down. The sun was sinking across Madaket harbor, behind Tuckernuck island; the wind was coming up again. He thought of Sheri and shrugged. It wasn't so much that she had slept with Frank, it was the fact that she had needed to. That was the real issue.

But still, something in Kevin refused to give up. If he was losing Sheri, he would lose her in spite of himself, not because of himself. If he had been blind before, he would learn to see. And if she still left, he would grow from the pain of it, like . . . like the bay scallop, which draws its nourishment from the mud and slime at the bottom of the sea.

He walked home in half the time it had taken him to cover the same distance that morning. Sheri heard him on the porch and opened the door. Seeing her there, he felt an impulse to shy away, despite his resolution to see things through.

"Hello," he said.

"Hi," she replied. She seemed no more certain of herself than he was. "What's in the bag?"

"A present for Sam."

"That was nice of you."

"I guess it's time to head on over to the party," he said. He vaguely felt it would be easier for them to be together around other people; he wasn't thinking clearly enough to realize that Frank and Suzanne would also be there.

"Are you sure we should go?" she asked.

"Why not?"

"I don't want to upset anyone."

"I think they'll be upset if we don't come."

Sheri turned her palms upside down, then let them drop. He had the power of having been wronged on his side. She brushed her hair and put on a jacket. He was waiting for her by the front door.

"Kevin," Sheri said, coming up to him and touching him on the chest, "I . . . I just want you to know that I don't feel very good about what I did."

"I'm not perfect either," he said curtly, and turned

and walked outside. Although he had vowed not to drive her farther away, he could not resist one more chance to use his emotional leverage.

As Sheri walked beside him in the darkness, she could feel his proud aloofness, cold and sharp as metal. She knew it concealed hurt, but she didn't have the strength to reach through it. Kevin guessed her thoughts and told himself silently that she mistook his unflinching honesty for aloofness.

The road to Russell and Mary's house was rutted and uneven. A few times Sheri stumbled, and he caught her but immediately pulled away again. It was very dark during the first part of the trip, but the eastern sky was slowly growing lighter before them. And as they came over a hill, the moon hung before them, just clear of the horizon. It was huge and slightly flattened at the top. Sheri saw it with a sense of distaste and wished it would go away.

The house was lit up and full of noise. They knocked on the kitchen door and waited a few minutes for someone to come, but no one answered. Everyone seemed to be farther inside. A car pulled into the driveway behind them and stopped. Footsteps crunched the gravel. Kevin pushed the door open, and they went inside. Colorful balloons were pinned to the wallboard in the kitchen. A cake box sat on the floor in a corner. Sheri mentally took a breath, as they walked on. They went about five feet into the living room and stopped.

They stood there, looking at the guests, and the noise level seemed to fall to almost nothing for a second, and then it rebounded with hysterical energy. At first Sheri thought everyone was looking at her. But she quickly realized they were looking past her. She half turned, and it all became clear: directly behind them in the doorway stood Suzanne. For a moment Suzanne's eyes fell upon Sheri, with their gentle, tremulous light. There was an innocent questioning in her gaze.

Instinctively, Sheri moved off to one side to let Suzanne by. Suzanne nodded with a smile toward Mary and Sam and walked past Sheri, erect and graceful. Kevin came up next to Sheri and put his hand on her arm.

Just then, the barbershop quartet bounded into the room, with the upbeat energy characteristic of them. They had on their usual outfits: blue shirts and white pants and red bow ties. The room grew quiet in expectation. Frank was frowning and looking at the floor. Then he hit low C, and the group launched into "Coney Island Baby." The song went along fine until they came to the part where Frank threw up his arms and said, "Drop that gun! I'll marry your daughter!" A wave of reaction swept across the room, like the steam thrown off when water is dashed against a hot stove. The group was thrown off balance; they kept on but were rushing to the end. Only a smattering of applause greeted the concluding chord. Hurriedly, as though they had just realized they were naked and had to do something to distract everyone's attention, they went right into "Chattanooga Choo Choo." As the lilting swing rhythm got going, Sam came out in front of the group and bent his knees and lifted his shoulders in time to the music. Mary had been working on this with him recently, trying to teach him to dance. But it seemed to her now that he was in an exposed and dangerous spot, and she went over to him, picked him up, and carried him over to the side of the room.

Normally the group would have sung several more songs, but it was clear that they shouldn't continue. Milton jogged over to Russell and returned with some party hats. They stuck the hats on their heads and began "Happy Birthday." The whole crowd joined in nervously, grateful for the release. There was applause and cheering, and the noise of the party came sweeping back to full volume. Frank stood talking idly to someone, fully aware that Suzanne was only a few feet away. He hadn't seen her since that morning; she had stayed away from the house all afternoon and come directly to the party.

Near Frank, but ignoring him, Kevin was exchanging pleasantries with Russell. Sheri was still at his side, not joining in the conversation. She found suddenly that she was crying. She turned her head to the wall so no one could see. Could anyone notice anything in such noise? She made her way back to the kitchen and outside into the moonlight. She walked down to the end of the driveway and stopped there, wondering if anyone had noticed, if Kevin had noticed.

Kevin had noticed, but before he could follow her, he had a mission to accomplish. He darted over to the side of the room and returned with his present. His path took him right past Frank, but they didn't look at each other; he walked right up to Sam and handed him the package. Excitedly, Sam pawed at the wrapping paper. With an assist from his father, he opened it. Russell saw what it was and let out a loud whoop.

"Thanks, Kevy. This is great!" he said. He held it up for others to see. It was a toy Yoda, seated on top of a miniature pickup truck.

Kevin saw Frank turn his head to look, and their eyes met, just briefly, for the first time since that morning. Frank looked away first.

Sam was waving the present over his head and laughing. Kevin turned back toward him, beaming with a pleased, shy expression. While he waited for a distraction which would allow him to leave inconspicuously, he talked to Mary and watched Sam open more presents.

His chance came when Sam finally grew overwrought from all the noise and excitement and began to cry. As Mary carried him off, Kevin slipped out through the kitchen. He found Sheri at the end of the driveway, leaning against a tree.

"I feel horrible," she said, and something in her voice was so honest and genuine that he felt a surge of feeling for her.

"I'm sorry I brought you," he said.

"Were you punishing me?"

"Not consciously. Let's go home."

He put his arm around her, and a tide of confused feelings rose within him. Together, they walked home. Although they had bright moonlight behind them now, they stumbled frequently—more than on their earlier trip in the dark. It seemed to Kevin that it was impossible to separate her actions from his; her mistakes sprang from his, and his from hers, as surely as if they were one four-legged, two-headed creature making its awkward way through the night.

Suzanne floated through the rest of the party without ever touching the ground. All the activity around her seemed curious and faintly comical. She was aware that people were looking at her and wondering about her, but their interest seemed quirky and inexplicable. She simply smiled at them and said whatever came into her head; it was easy to smile and look happy when nothing quite touched her. And while nothing touched her, it seemed that she had a superior insight into the people and the situation. She saw how embarrassed Frank was when he sang the line about marrying someone's daughter. Of course he felt that: he was having trouble with the idea of growing older. She saw how concerned Mary looked, and this made her smile too: Mary was concerned because this was her child's first birthday party, and everything had to be just so. She saw Kevin slip outside to be with Sheri and thought how nice it was that unmarried people could be so loyal.

The one element missing in her observations was herself. She simply didn't believe that everyone could be so concerned about her, especially when they had so many problems of their own. Poor Russell; his drinking was starting up again. She saw him finish one beer, then another, and once he had to grab onto a chair for balance. And his friend Roger, the unbalanced one, the one who had threatened to shoot someone with a shotgun last winter. And Sammy, her brother, who was lonely because he alienated everyone and had taken up with that mean, confused woman.

Most of all she was concerned about little Sam, since it was his birthday but he wasn't having a good time at all. The child was obviously confused by the noise and upset by all the commotion. He was sitting on his mother's lap in a corner, crying and crying. Suzanne floated over toward him. Sam's face grew larger and larger in her vision until it seemed to hover before her like some great hot-air balloon; he had come to the age where cuteness in the baby becomes ugliness in the child.

Mary smiled ruefully up at her, and Suzanne felt herself smiling back in an automatic response. She was conscious of the power she held over Mary; she had the feeling that she could do anything and Mary would still adore her. She almost wanted to test it—to say something cruel just to see what Mary would do—but even in her numb, floating state cruelty was foreign to her. Still, she felt the impulse, and it registered in her mind for later review.

She leaned over Mary and said, "I can picture this house filling up with little children."

Mary, looked up, her eyes filling with tears. Suzanne touched her on the arm.

"Did I say something wrong?"

Mary closed her eyes. Tears were rolling down her cheeks. She shook her head.

"Now, Mary, children always get upset at parties," Suzanne said.

Mary shook her head again; that wasn't why she was crying.

Suzanne's mind considered further, in its curiously detached mode. "If it's Russell, I wouldn't be too concerned," she said. "He'll come out of it."

Again, Mary shook her head.

"Well, then, what is it?" Suzanne asked.

Mary tried to speak a few times and couldn't. Finally she said, "It's not for me. It's for you."

Suzanne gave Mary a funny look and floated off toward the center of the room. Her brother Sammy was arguing with Jack.

"They're going to be the death of this island," Sammy was saying, in his emphatic, abrasive way. His arm was draped around his new lady friend. "Bringing in all that outside wealth, buying up everything."

"Maybe that's for the best," Jack replied speculatively, looking at a balloon that had come free and was drifting slowly down from the ceiling. "At least if they do it with class." His words had a sarcastic edge; he knew Sammy would rise to the bait.

"This poor island can't take much more class like they've got. Already they've raised prices so high that none of the kids growing up today are ever going to be able to afford a place to live."

"The developers haven't raised the prices." Jack

snorted. "The economics of the entire East Coast have done it. How many places are there like Nantucket, just a half hour by plane from the wealthiest area of the world? Of course prices are going up."

"It's gotta stop sometime," Sammy said.

"I don't see it hurting you. Did the clothing business suffer last summer?"

"No, it was a pretty good year," Sammy replied. "But it's the day-trippers who buy clothing, not the rich developers who come in here and jack up prices."

"The day-trippers?" Jack asked. "You mean the tourists?"

"I think 'day-tripper' is a more descriptive term."

"Less negative, perhaps—which suits your purpose. But a rose by any other name, you know. Ah, the day-trippers. Now there are the people who are going to be the death of the island."

"That's an asinine remark. The day-trippers don't hurt anybody. They come in, rent their mopeds, buy a few things from the stores, and leave. What harm is there in that? It's the developers who are tearing the island apart."

"And who buys up all the developments?"

"You tell me."

"The day-trippers, that's who. They come here for a day or two and like it so much they decide to purchase a little place of their own. If it weren't for them, there wouldn't be any developers."

"That's not the point."

"I don't know, Sammy," Jack said. "I think you got a double standard, my boy."

"You'd be upset, too, if someone was trying to buy your church."

"One of the advantages of Catholicism is that the church can't be bought off," Jack remarked.

161

"It isn't a question of being bought off," Sammy said. "It's a question of survival."

"That's what the locals have been saying all these years, Sam, as they keep selling more and more land to developers."

Sammy shook his finger at Jack. "You see, you finally admit it—it is the developers who are causing all the trouble."

Jack saw Suzanne then, and he raised his eyebrows and shook his head as a comment on the intractable behavior of her brother. Suzanne felt herself smiling in return, a dazed, complicit smile, and as she did so she saw Jack look at her with concern. She drifted away from him and found herself behind Russell and Roger. They were both sipping a beer and laughing loudly.

"I tell you, Roger, you really got me going the other day when you gave me that PT-boat line," Russell said.

"Found a sensitve spot, did I?" Roger replied. As always, his hair and beard were uncombed and scraggly, and his eyes burned.

"I wouldn't let everybody talk to me like that." Russell held up the can of beer before his face and examined it with a serious expression.

"You gotta put up with me; you gotta put up with Mike Hussey. Which is worse?"

"I think you're a little easier to put up with, Rog," Russell said. "But still, you ain't easy."

Watching them, Suzanne had the feeling that she had become invisible, that she could float around the room unobserved and learn all the things that people normally hid from her. But just then Roger turned and saw her. Russell followed his look and saw her too, but before either of them could speak, Suzanne turned. She found herself beside Frank and Milton. Milton was talking to Frank in a quiet voice, very earnestly. Frank was frowning and looking at the floor. Milton saw Suzanne and looked up immediately and smiled. Frank continued frowning at the floor. Milton was saying something to her, but the words weren't making any sense. Milton knew she wasn't herself. He stopped and said, "Franky, I think you better take Suzanne home."

"You want to go home, honey?" Frank asked.

"Yes," Suzanne said, feeling a sudden desperate urge to leave. She followed Frank into the kitchen.

During the car ride home, Suzanne felt herself drifting back down to solid ground, like a balloon with a slow leak. The unhappiness of her situation rose up around her. She couldn't begin to conceive of the future. What Frank would do didn't even present itself in her mind as a concern; what he had done was all that mattered. But it wasn't exactly what he had done. It was more the attitude behind his actions.

Even in her present state, Suzanne was as always highly conscious of Frank's feelings. She and Frank didn't talk as they drove home, but she was aware of his mood simply from the way he drove. In the jerky way he took the corners she could feel his confusion and bewildered defiance; in his occasional hesitation on the gas pedal she thought she sensed a small opening, a glimmer of regret.

While she couldn't think about the future, she knew his affair with Sheri, or whatever it was, couldn't go on. If he didn't bring it up (and she doubted he would), she knew she would have to say something to him.

They pulled into the driveway and got out. Woolly clouds flew across the face of the moon; the wind was rising. The shrubbery blew silver and dark as the light wavered, fell, then returned. Suzanne felt her heart steeling.

They went into the kitchen. The overhead light gleamed coldly on the polished surface of the loom. Everything familiar to her, everything she loved, seemed strange and in danger of slipping away. Frank walked on ahead of her. She couldn't let him leave the room without settling something; he was already at the door. She had to act.

"Frank, stop."

His stride hesitated, halted. He turned slowly to her.

"I want to be your culler from now on," she said, listening to the ring of her voice as she spoke.

He frowned and looked at the floor. He waited so long that she wondered if he was ever going to reply. Finally he said, "Umm-huh," and turned to leave the room.

"Frank," she said. He stopped again. "Are you going to tell her, or shall I?"

"I'll tell her." He turned again to leave.

"Don't you think you should tell her now?"

Frank turned back to her one more time, and she saw he was angry. "They're all asleep over there. Morning will be good enough."

"I don't want her coming here in the morning. Call her now," Suzanne insisted, surprised at her firmness.

"It's too late, Suzanne."

"Then I'll do it."

She walked over to the phone and opened their red address book. She found the number, in Frank's writing, and wondered how she could have been so blind: Frank's handwriting was normally quick and sloppy, but he had entered Sheri's number with care and grace. Suzanne picked up the phone and dialed. She heard it ring once. Then she knew she couldn't go through with it. She was about to put the phone down; but before she could, it was wrenched out of her grasp.

"Hello, Sheri," Frank was saying. "This is Frank. We . . . I guess we won't be needing you anymore on the boat."

Suzanne was close enough to hear Sheri's voice, small but nevertheless distinct.

"I guess I expected this," Sheri said.

"I'll mail you your check for last week."

"Please don't bother," Sheri said.

"No bother. Goodbye, then." Frank hung up.

"Of course you'll send her the check," Suzanne said. Now that the phone call had been made, she felt self-righteously protective of Sheri.

Frank turned and walked out of the room, and this time Suzanne knew that nothing she could say would make him stop. She sat down at the table and cupped her hands under her chin. She felt unclean and ugly and never so undeserving of love as now.

They lay in bed next to each other, without talking or touching. Suzanne was thinking that she had always been attracted to Frank for the distance he kept from her—not because she needed distance herself, or wanted room in which to operate, but because his distance had seemed a sign of substance. More accessible men always seemed shallow, lacking in belief in themselves, while men who kept to themselves seemed to have hidden reserves. But now Suzanne wondered. She thought about Kevin and Russell: each distant in his own way, and each in his way a man of substance. But now it seemed they had substance despite being distant, not because of it. Kevin was distant because he was brittle and selfish; Russell was distant because he was confused and taken in by his own bluff. And Frank? What caused the distance in him? She thought for a while but came to no conclusion. She couldn't tell. She knew him too well to make a judgment.

And so she would just have to wait and see what happened. Waiting. She thought of the day on Tucker-nuck when Frank proposed to her. That time of waiting was different—a doorway then, a wall now. But there was nothing else to do: if she tried to break down the wall, the whole structure might collapse. So she turned her back on Frank and tried to sleep, although she knew by his breathing that he was still awake too.

CHAPTER 11

Monday morning was gray and windy. Suzanne woke at five thirty. Frank was already up and about, moving quietly. She could smell coffee. She dressed and went to the kitchen to cook breakfast. She fried some eggs and then, thinking of how much Frank would like it, she put on some bacon too. The morning ritual brought back good feelings. She remembered his stories about going out scalloping as a boy of eight or nine, how the best part of it was the big breakfast his mother would fix for him. This early in the morning, her hurt and resentment had not had time to form. She hoped they wouldn't: she hoped she could hold them at bay. It was like trying to carry a bucket of cement balanced on the end of a long pole.

She placed the food on the table, and Frank took his seat and began to eat silently. She felt almost tender toward him now, remembering all the mornings they had risen together before dawn. But she didn't want to think too much, or her feelings would turn bitter.

"Coffee," he said, and without speaking she poured him a cup. The bottom had burned and had a bitter smell. He drank it without comment.

"Umm-huh," he said when he finished. They pulled

on their boots and oilers. It felt almost companionable, being together again in the early morning. But she had to keep her mental balance.

They went outside. The wind was stronger than she had expected. The temperature was brisk, in the upper 30s. There was still a feeling of autumn in the air—a sense of pumpkins and leaves, a hard, crisp tinge. She had to take in all these sensations very carefully, keeping her balance just right.

She bent over and put their lunch in the back of the truck.

"Hi!" A young woman's voice sounded in the air behind them, and Suzanne stiffened. How dare she come here this morning?

But when she turned, she saw it was Heather.

Heather was dressed for her gardening work in old jeans, a hooded sweatshirt, and low-cut boots. She was scowling; Suzanne thought the expression somehow made her look like Frank.

She walked up to Frank, who was setting a line in the back of the truck.

"Dad," she said, stopping a few feet from him and waiting for him to turn around.

Frank turned to her. "Hi, honey," he said. "Why up so early?"

She ignored his pleasantry. "I didn't hear the rumor until late last night. Or is it more than a rumor?"

"I don't know what you're talking about." Frank turned and got into the truck.

But Heather wasn't going to let him get away so easily. "That's the real reason Mom was crying, isn't it?" Heather demanded of him through the window.

"Come on, Suzanne, get in the car," Frank said.

"I can't believe you would do something like that,

Dad," Heather said. Tears were in her eyes. She looked toward him a moment, searchingly; his eyes remained averted. She turned and walked away.

Looking in through the window, Suzanne saw Frank shrink into himself. She felt an impulse to move toward him, and then an equal and opposite impulse to hold back. It occurred to her then, in a moment of clarity, that the worst effect of the episode on Tuckernuck would be the way it distanced Frank from the family.

She climbed into the truck. Frank was behind the steering wheel. As always, he poured himself a cup of coffee while he waited for the truck to warm up, but this time his hands trembled. Suzanne sat watching as in a dream. Some pressure was building and building inside her, and she knew suddenly that she couldn't take it anymore.

"I can't go, Frank," she said, and opened the door and stepped outside. She just needed to be away from him. She walked over to the picket fence and stood there, and she didn't even have it in her to cry. She stood there and watched the first beams of sunlight in the treetops.

Behind her, Frank walked back to the house, his head bowed.

She stayed there until the sunlight had descended the entire length of the tree and spread in swaths across the ground beside her. Then she went inside. Frank wasn't in the kitchen; he was probably downstairs in his shop.

Suzanne took off her oilers, hung them on the peg in the hallway, and sat down at the loom. Sunlight blew in fitfully onto the wall, dancing across the framed quotation that hung beside the loom. It was the passage

169

from *Moby Dick;* Heather had come across it in school a few years back and typed it out for her mother.

The straight warp of necessity, not to be swerved from its ultimate course—its every alternating vibration, indeed, only tending to that; free will still free to ply her shuttle between given threads; and chance, though restrained in its play within the right lines of necessity, and sideways in its motions directed by free will, though thus prescribed to by both, chance by turns rules either, and has the last featuring blow at events.

Suzanne had never before given much thought to the quotation, but remembering the sermon she read it again, and it took on new meaning. Some things had to happen; some things could be decided by an individual's free will; and other things simply came about by chance. All those factors together made up the fabric of events.

In other words, Frank's actions on Tuckernuck had only partly been the result of his free will. He had decided to do it, yes—but only in one particular situation, which had been brought about by a combination of necessity and chance. In another situation, he might have come to a different decision.

What did that mean about his feelings for her? That they should not be doubted, since his actions had been largely out of his control? Or that they should be doubted totally, since they too had been brought about largely by necessity and chance, and only partly through his free will?

And what about her feelings for him? Wasn't she only partly responsible for them, since so much was determined by necessity and chance? Didn't this mean, in the final analysis, that she was no better than he?

Suzanne began to work the shuttle but soon stopped. It seemed pointless to sit here several hours a day, controlling a private universe of yarn, finding a peace that was only possible because it was artificial. She wondered how much her weaving was an excuse to keep herself from being truly involved with other people. Oh, she did help people sometimes, she knew that; but in her present mood it seemed to her that the help she gave was a subtle form of manipulation, allowing her to be loved or admired without being truly involved. She always maintained a slight distance. Never had that distance been so clear to her as now, when she couldn't reach out to anyone else in her need. She had busied herself too often with the fabric of other people's lives; the fabric of her own life was weak and worn thin.

Frank, working in the shop on a new door, was beginning to feel the unfairness of it all. Sure, he had been attracted to the girl; what healthy male wouldn't be? And sure, he had liked her, too. But things never would have come to this point if it hadn't been for a strange series of circumstances that were out of his control. It wasn't as if he had tried to run the boat aground; it was just that his eyes were getting weaker and the shoals out there to the east of Tuckernuck were moving around like a bastard. In a way, it was the getting older (his weakening eyes), and the passage of time (the moving shoals) that had run them aground. And who can control time and old age?

Besides, the whole thing hadn't been his idea, anyway. When he and Sheri got to the house he was perfectly content to fall asleep in the chair, until she woke him up stark naked. It didn't really change his overall feelings toward Suzanne. But try to explain that to her and see how far he would get. Suzanne would never believe it was just a fluke.

The problem was, she was too good and too sincere. He knew she had never given herself to anyone but him and never would. It was the way she was. But did that mean he had no leeway at all, no freedom to act a little irresponsibly from time to time?

And the other thing was, he genuinely liked Sheri. Not that he had ever intended things to go this far—but he had a special admiration for her. Why should that be wrong? What was wrong with liking someone?

But all his reflections skirted around one central issue: *he* had been wrong. He had hurt Suzanne. No matter how much he thought intellectually that good and bad were relative concepts, he felt inside himself that they were not. No matter how much he told himself he should be allowed to like Sheri, he knew he shouldn't have done what he did. He knew it but didn't want to face it.

He puttered around in the shop without getting much accomplished. The clock said seven fifteen. There was still time to get to the West End; he could go by himself and get a single limit. He might as well; he'd feel better on the water. He walked out to the truck and remembered he'd forgotten his oilers. He went in the shop to get them, and when he came back to the truck, Suzanne was there.

"I'll go with you if you want," she said.

He nodded to the door, telling her to get in.

It all came back effortlessly for Suzanne, like driving a standard shift. She stood at her accustomed place on the bow side of the culling board as Frank brought in the dredges. A whole network of small sensory details fell back into place: the way pieces of seaweed and

172

beads of water blew in her face as the line pulled taut out of the water; the peculiarly fresh but dank odor of eelgrass; the subtle but unmistakable lightness of a dead scallop in her hand; the pull on her shoulder as she leaned over the side to wash a basket of adults. She could cull as fast as ever, and she found relief in the quick, simple rhythm of the work. Pull off the eelgrass, shove the bad scallops over the side, toss the good ones into the metal basket on the board. Keep working to the right, toward the side, continually pushing the junk off the edge. She pushed overboard mountains of crabs, conchs, starfish, old bottles, pieces of timber, toadfish. But the metal baskets were also filling up fast with the keepers. She kept emptying basket after basket into the blue bushel boxes. Two baskets made a level box, but that was never enough for Frank, and she knew how to pull apart the sides of a box and shake it to bring the level down. If you worked at it you could shake it down far enough to accept another half basket. Suzanne wondered in passing if Sheri had shaken down the boxes, and then she made a conscious effort not to think about the girl.

After she had filled five boxes, Suzanne stopped for a rest. Five boxes was the halfway point, and she and Frank had always taken a break then. But when she bent down under the culling board and brought out the boiled eggs and small cans of V-8 juice for their snack, Frank gave her a funny look.

"What're you doing?" he asked.

"Snack time," she said.

"Already?"

"We filled five."

Frank looked puzzled. "I guess I lost track of the tows," he said. "I thought we only did three."

"We did."

"Hmph."

"That's a box and two-thirds a tow. What's so strange about that?"

"We were only getting a little over a box here the other day."

Frank bent down and looked at the boxes arranged neatly under the board.

"You're crowning 'em up good? Yep, look pretty good." He stood back up, pulled the tab off the top of the can, and drained the juice in one gulp. He peeled his egg, looking off over the water. "Well, Suzanne, I guess it just shows how much better an experienced culler is," he said.

Suzanne felt her cheeks burning and wondered if it was the wind or the sun.

"It won't be that easy, Frank," she said.

He remained silent, still looking off over the water.

The rest of the day went slower. The tide began to fall, and the dredges picked up more seed, fewer adults. By the tenth tow they only had eight boxes.

Suzanne found that she was able to cull off the board completely between dredges. This was unusual; in the old days Frank had brought in the dredges too fast for her to keep up. She watched him and saw that he was pausing longer than usual between each one. At one point he sat down on the gunwale for a minute, his head lowered.

"Are you okay?" she asked.

"Fine," he said, getting up.

He brought in the rest of the dredges without pausing, but after he set the next tow, Suzanne saw that he was breathing more heavily than normal.

"Maybe we shouldn't bother to get ten if we don't get them with this tow," she said.

"This should do it," he replied.

"If it doesn't, let's go in, okay?"

He waved his hand at her.

Suzanne sat down on a box, waiting for the end of the tow. The sun was falling in the western sky, behind Tuckernuck. She saw the boxlike shape of the Hussey house. It stood out against the silver sky with eerie clarity; she could see the individual bricks in the chimney. Nearby, some swans had finished their feeding and were rising from the water in a slow spiral. It reminded her of the waterspouts that lift whole boats and crews up into the air, never to return.

She looked up suddenly. The boat was veering off toward the shallows offshore.

"Frank!" she said. He was sitting with his head lowered between his knees.

He stood up. "I'm okay," he said. He whipped the wheel around and brought the boat back on course.

"What's wrong?"

"Just a little tired."

Her sympathy burned brown at the edges. He was playing with her, trying to buy his way out with the purchase of her pity.

At the completion of the next tow, they had only nine boxes. But without putting up a protest, Frank steered back toward Madaket harbor. In the late-afternoon light the land mass seemed to hover a few feet above the water, drifting in and out of focus.

The air was noticeably cooler now, and Suzanne huddled under the board for warmth. They were past the shoals, and to avoid the wind in his face, Frank steered facing the stern, looking forward only occasionally. Suzanne watched his back. He looked inaccessible and vulnerable all at once.

CHAPTER 12

Mary spent most of Monday morning at the new house, cleaning up the mess left by Sam's birthday party. As she worked she thought almost constantly about Suzanne. Was Suzanne sitting at home now, brooding, while Frank was off scalloping with Sheri? The more Mary thought about it, the worse she felt. When she returned to the apartment after cleaning, she tried calling Suzanne, but there was no answer. When she tried again, about noon, Mike answered. In a surly voice he told her no one was home.

While Sam took his nap, Mary set to work on a lightship basket. She had made more than thirty over the past year, and the work required little conscious attention—so little, in fact, that she sometimes drifted off to sleep over her work. It happened again today; her head nodded little by little, and her hands stopped moving. She didn't know how long she slept, but she woke up with a start; the phone was ringing. She jumped out of her chair, feeling unattached in time and space.

"Hello, Mary?" a woman's voice inquired. It was a pretty voice; for a moment Mary thought it might be Suzanne's, but it was too hesitant, too unsure.

"Yes?" she replied. The world was just beginning to come into focus around her.

"This is Sheri. I'm sorry to bother you. I . . . I need to talk to someone. May I come over?"

"Of course," Mary said, responding to the misery in the voice before her hostile judgments had time to form.

"Could I come now?"

"Sure. Sure. Do you know where we live?"

"I think Kevin mentioned it once. By North Wharf."

"Yes. Number seventeen."

"Thank you, Mary. I'll be there in a few minutes."

As Mary set the phone back down, the weight of her judgment descended, and she wondered what in the world Sheri expected of her.

She went around cleaning up the house, feeling as if she were preparing for battle.

Half an hour later there was a knock on the door. With conscious, deliberate steps, Mary walked over to the door and opened it. Sheri was standing partway up the front steps. She was wearing a blue scarf on her head, tied in back, and an old, oversized sweater that looked as though it might have belonged to her father. She smiled up at Mary quickly, then bowed her head and walked into the apartment.

"Would you like something to drink? A cup of tea?" Mary asked, vaguely annoyed that Sheri always managed to look stylish no matter what she wore.

"Oh. No. No, thanks," Sheri said, as though she had never even considered the possibility that someone might offer her tea at a time like this. "But . . . please have some yourself if you want."

Sheri sat down on the sagging old sofa by the window. With the light behind her, the front of her face was in shadow, but Mary could see by the set of her jaw that she was very upset.

Mary waited for her to speak, and when it seemed that Sheri wasn't going to begin, she said, "Did you go out today?"

"What? No. No, it would have been impossible. After what . . . I can't go scalloping with Frank any more."

Mary made no reply. It seemed to her that Sheri's speech was strangely affected, and she thought it was from pride rather than embarrassment. She was content now to sit in silence.

"I just hope that Suzanne isn't too hurt by what happened," Sheri said suddenly, looking down at the sofa.

"Why should she be hurt?" Mary blurted out. Sheri looked up. Her silence encouraged Mary to go on and speak her mind. "You people come from off-island and buy up the land and build your vacation houses and sleep with our husbands. Don't you think she knows better than to be hurt?"

Sheri stared at her. Mary sat still, her arms crossed, still too angry to be sorry for what she had said.

Sheri replied slowly, in a small, distinct voice, "I want to know what I can do to help."

"Don't you think you're a little late?" Mary replied, her anger rising again.

"I don't know," Sheri said, taken off guard.

"What help do you think you can be?" Mary asked her.

Sheri thought a few moments. "I appreciate your candor," she said, in her slow, distinct voice. "Most people wouldn't say what they really thought." Her face turned to the light, and Mary saw real pain in it.

"You've caused a lot of misery," Mary said, but her voice was softer now.

"I'm sorry," Sheri said. "Maybe I don't belong on Nantucket."

"A lot of the people who are here don't belong here. Especially single people."

"I'm not exactly single," Sheri said. "Although I don't know about that now, either." She looked down at the floor again.

"How is Kevin?"

"I really don't know."

"What do you mean?"

"He's changing somehow, but I don't know how."

"He knows about . . . what happened, of course?"

"Oh, yes. He's no dummy."

"I thought he handled himself well last night."

"He can surprise me. He didn't handle himself very well at our party."

"He did better than Russell did," Mary snorted and shook her head.

"You know, you Nantucketers are very nice people," Sheri said. "You really are. I wish . . . you didn't know me in this light."

"What are you going to do about a job now?" Mary had picked up her basket and was weaving again.

"I don't know."

"Maybe you could open somewhere."

"I wasn't very good at that. I tried it once."

"You could learn. You don't get it the first time."

"Kevin did."

"Some people learn slower."

"Oh, I'm a slow learner, all right."

Sheri stood up and walked over to the saltwater aquarium, which was on a table not far from the sofa. A hermit crab made its way slowly along the gravel bottom, carrying its borrowed conch shell; near its mouth, a series of arms rippled ceaselessly. A shrimp flew backward with quick flips of its translucent body. An eel lay coiled in a leafy plant; a fat, squat fish sat despondently nearby. A lobster no longer than Sheri's little finger stalked a tiny minnow.

"Russell caught everything in there when he was out scalloping," Mary told her. "Lobsters, crabs, conch, the toadfish—he picked them all off the culling board."

"It's wonderful," Sheri said, kneeling down by it and letting the blue light wash over her. The eel slithered off to another corner.

"Sam loves it."

"I'll bet he can sit and watch it for an hour."

"His attention span isn't quite that long. But he loves it."

"It must be nice to be married and have a child," Sheri said, turning to Mary. "It seems to me like such . . . an uphill struggle to get to that point. To be established in your life, and just live from then on."

"There are always struggles," Mary said, looking back down at her weaving.

"But you take them on from a different point. You have a base to work from."

"Sometimes it seems like the world has closed in on you."

"You have a world." Sheri looked at the aquarium again; for the first time, she noticed her reflection peering back at her. "I've been thinking about going to see Suzanne and apologizing," she said. "Do you think that would be a good idea?"

Mary looked over at her and shook her head no.

"You're right," Sheri said after a moment. "It would only make me feel better."

"I think you just have to go on."

"I have a long way to go," Sheri said, "before I get to the point where you are." Her gaze turned back toward the aquarium with longing. "You know, my father always wanted to have an aquarium, but he never did." She shrugged her shoulders. "Thank you for letting me talk." She rose and said goodbye, carrying a burden of feeling that seemed disproportionate to her slight frame. Watching her go, Mary realized that things were larger and more complicated than she had let herself think.

The conversation at the shanty that evening was about Frank Hussey and his former culler.

"You can bet he put it to her," confirmed one of the openers, a large, brawny young man of mixed Portuguese and black descent. He shook his head and showed his white teeth. "I'd love to rip into a woman like that. Slender, like a racehorse."

"I bet his wife ain't too happy about it," someone else said.

"Wives never are," a third opener added. "But hell, a wife is like a boat."

"Like a what?"

"Like a boat. A boat is a hole in the water that sucks up all your money and gives nothing back. A wife is the same thing, but on land."

"Women always start off hot, and then they cool off. They get what they deserve."

"Not a woman like that Sheri," the first one argued. "She wouldn't cool off. You seen those tight blue jeans she peels on every morning? That girl's got one beautiful ass. She wants it. She wants it bad."

At that moment, Mike Hussey came inside, and the shanty fell silent. As usual, he was scowling, and his pupils were dilated to an unnatural size. He took off his jacket and walked over to the line of pegs where the openers hung their plastic aprons. He swore loudly and walked outside, slamming the door behind him. Some of the others exchanged looks.

"He's mad 'cause his dad got it instead of him," commented the large, talkative opener.

Mike came back with his apron, which he had left outside in his beat-up old pickup truck. He walked over to Russell's bench, looked at the scallops, and swore loudly. He knocked a few scallops off the bench.

"This is trash from First Bend," he told no one in particular. "Why'd Russell leave the frigging Horseshed for this?"

"I heard him say Horseshed was getting mucked up from all the other boats," someone said.

"He could do better than this. These things have pencil erasers in 'em." Mike found a plastic trash can for the shells and guts and started opening.

Soon Roger came inside with his scallops. "Long day out there, boys. Long day," he announced. Mike swore again.

"What's the matter with you?" Roger asked.

"None of your frigging business," Mike said.

"He's upset 'cause his dad got a piece instead of him," one of the openers repeated.

Roger went outside for the rest of his scallops.

"That's it, ain't it, Mike?" someone teased Mike.

Mike didn't answer. He continued opening in silence.

"A man deserves a woman like that," the loquacious opener went on. "He works hard all day, he deserves a sweet young honey."

"Bet your mom don't like it too much, though," someone said.

"Leave her out of this," Mike said.

Roger came inside again. "Leave who out of what?" he asked. It grew quiet in the shanty; the only sound was the click of scallops on the bench as they opened and shut their shells, trying to breathe.

"His mother," the opener said.

"He's got a damn nice mother," Roger said. "Why should she be left out of anything?"

"Because I said so," Mike shouted at Roger, turning toward him.

"Don't shout at me, punk," Roger yelled back. "You should learn a little respect for your mother. She's the only person on this whole goddam island who can put up with you."

Mike came toward Roger in his stoned fury. He strode right up to Roger and straight-armed him down onto the floor. Roger picked himself up and leaped at Mike. They rolled onto a bench and over the other side. Scallops slid smashing to the floor. The other openers watched silently, keeping their distance.

Roger rose to his feet.

"You die, dog!" he screamed. He picked up a window weight which was lying on a sill.

Mike grabbed a shovel and circled in toward Roger. He took a swipe at Roger and missed. Roger tried to move into striking range with his window weight, but Mike shoved him away with the point of the shovel. Roger raised the weight, getting ready to strike, and Mike slammed it out of his hands with the shovel. The weight slid under one of the benches.

Roger retreated to the far side of the bench, looking for a chance to duck underneath and retrieve the weight. Mike pursued him, grasping the shovel in two hands like a baseball bat.

A large shape filled the door. A huge voice boomed out.

"Mike, drop that shovel! Drop it! Now!" the voice ordered.

Mike glanced over toward Russell, but his grip on the shovel remained firm.

"Drop it, Mike, or I'll break your goddam neck!" Russell said. He moved in toward Mike.

Just then Roger lunged under the table for the weight. Mike swung at him and caught him on the back, up near the neck, with the blade of the shovel. Roger crumpled to the ground. Russell leaped the remaining distance. He ripped into Mike's face with an elbow smash, and Mike slid the length of the room, slamming into a box of unopened scallops. The shovel clattered away along the floor. Mike stood up, facing Russell. A trickle of blood ran down his face, the width of fine-spun wool. Roger lay on the floor, moaning.

"You take one step toward me and I'll kill you," Russell told Mike.

"I don't wanna fight you," Mike said. "It's that asshole."

"You get out of here now," Russell told him. "And don't you come back. Ever. And if this guy's hurt"—he gestured toward Roger—"I'm gonna come get you. You understand?"

"I don't have any quarrel with you."

"Get out. Now."

Mike turned and left. Russell looked after him a minute, shaking his head.

"You try to help a kid, and look what happens," he said. He knelt down beside Roger.

"You okay, Rog?" he asked.

Roger was still moaning.

"Christ. Help me get him to the hospital," Russell said. The openers crowded around. They carried Roger outside and laid him down in the back of Russell's old Toyota.

Kevin and Sheri had little to say to each other that day. They had made a kind of temporary truce the previous evening after the party, but too much remained unresolved for normal conversation. Sheri felt that Kevin was glowering at her, and during dinner, for some reason, he kept glancing at the top of her head. Finally he just shook his head and put his fork down on the plate.

"What's the matter?" she asked.

"Will you please take off that scarf?"

"Why?"

"You don't have to do penance, you know."

"What's that have to do with the scarf?"

Kevin waved his arm and ate on in silence.

"How'd the practicing go this afternoon?" she asked. He had only played for about an hour.

"Okay."

"You beginning to feel ready for the audition?"

He didn't answer.

"You know, Kevin, you tell me I don't need to do penance, and then you won't talk to me."

The phone rang, and Kevin jumped up and answered it. Sheri listened to the glum tones in his voice. She couldn't figure out what it was about, but she knew it was something bad.

"What happened?" she asked when Kevin hung up.

"One of Russell's openers got in a brawl. Russell fired him, and now he needs some help."

"I'll go too," Sheri said, standing up.

"Don't you ever stop?" Kevin asked her.

"What?"

"I said, Don't you ever stop?"

"Stop what?"

"Trying to butt your way into everything I do."

"Well, I—" she began, but before she could go on Kevin left the room. She smashed a wineglass on the floor and stood there, head in her hands. Kevin came back with his jacket and closed the front door behind him.

The night was calm, clear and cold. As Kevin came closer to the shanty, he was greeted by the stench of scallop guts that had not yet been carted away. The truck was overflowing with shells and guts; apparently the whole process had been interrupted by the fight.

Inside, the mood was quiet and tense. The police had been by to ask questions and had just left. Only about ten openers were still at the shanty, working away in silence. Instead of the normal blast of music, a small transistor radio played softly. There were still afterwaves of shock in the air.

Kevin found an apron and a knife and started opening. He had the procedure down to three steps: insert the knife, pull off the guts, flip out the eye. He found a certain satisfaction in gauging his rhythm against the opener in the next bay and finding that he was faster, though he was quite tired—tired to the point of forgetting the problems that had been occupying him so much.

One of the openers finished for the day, poured his bucket of shucked scallops onto the scale, and hosed off his plastic apron. He left, taking the radio with him, and in the sudden quiet the labors of the remaining openers filled the room. As the scallop shells fell away into the trash cans, there was an incessant clicking, like icicles breaking and falling. From time to time there was a rumble as another box of scallops was emptied onto the bench. Icelike, too, were the blasts of cold air that came roaring into the room every time an opener dragged a full trash can outside to dump the shells.

When Kevin closed his eyes, he could almost imagine he was standing at the edge of the great glacier that had deposited Nantucket in the middle of the ocean, centuries and centuries ago, and then melted away to form the underground aquifer that supplied water to the island. He could imagine the glacier traveling slowly southward, while the ice rumbled and cracked and snapped under its burden of sand, mud, and rock. The broken bits of shell and scallop guts under his feet were like the thawed debris of the glacier; the blasts of Atlantic night air blew over him as they had blown over the island for aeons.

Then, by a curious juxtaposition made possible by his combined tiredness and keenness, Kevin thought of Russell's son Sam—so young compared to a global event so old—and wondered how in the world Sam would ever understand the creation of the island. With a quick leap of imagination characteristic of him, he saw the creation of Nantucket in terms of a children's story. He would write it down when he went home that night.

Russell stayed at the hospital with Roger most of the evening. He came back to the shanty about eight thirty and found that Kevin was almost done.

"Unbelievable, Kevy," he said. His face looked longer than usual—horselike, beaten—and he kept shaking his head, quite unconsciously.

"How's Roger?"

"Bad. Real bad." Russell wouldn't say anything more.

Kevin finished up and carried the white plastic bucket full of scallop eyes over to the scales. They weighed in at 63 pounds, by far the lowest total Russell and Kevin had brought in on any day so far. Russell came over, looked at the scale, and shook his head again.

"Well, tomorrow's another day," he said. "See you at six thirty. Hey, you want a ride home?"

"That's okay. I'll walk."

"Man, you're some opener," Russell said.

"Years of practice," Kevin replied, without bitterness. He walked outside. The waning moon, three quarters full, was rising in the east. He thought of Sheri then and felt a pang of remorse. An idea came to him, and he decided to talk to her about it.

When Kevin came home, he found Sheri in the back room she used as a studio.

"Hi."

"Hi," she replied. Her tone showed she was not happy with him, but didn't feel much ground to stand on in a fight. The scarf was still on her head.

"I'm sorry I left you like that."

"It doesn't matter." Smiling her wry, self-deprecating smile, she stepped back and looked at her picture. It was a new one—of a seagull tilting back its head and letting out a cry.

"It does matter. I won't do it again."

"You're very serious tonight."

"The mood at the shanty was pretty glum. Mike hit Roger with a shovel, and I guess Roger was hurt pretty badly."

"I wonder who will open for Russell now?"

"I was thinking about that. I think I'll offer to do it."

"You can't cull for Russell all day and then open. It would be too long a day."

"I wouldn't cull."

"Who would?"

"You."

"Oh, no, Kevin. That wouldn't work," she said, instantly understanding that he had been getting at this all along.

"It would work fine."

"I don't think so," she said, turning her head away.

"Why not?"

"Because." She turned back to him. "But thank you for thinking of it, Kevin."

He came over and hugged her, but as they embraced she gazed off into the distance.

Kevin went into the living room, took out a pencil and paper, and wrote down his story.

How Nantucket Came to Be

A long time ago, there was a father glacier and a mother glacier and a baby glacier who lived way up north near the North Pole. The baby glacier loved to play in the mud and sand. But his mother told him no; he was getting himself all dirty. So the baby glacier, who was very stubborn about having his own way, ran away from home.

Not caring where he went, the baby glacier headed south. He ran across Canada and New England, and then, as he was crossing the mountains of New Hampshire, he slipped and fell. He slid all the way to the shores of Massachusetts. But he was traveling so fast he couldn't stop there; he slid right on out into the Atlantic Ocean. He barely had time to reach down and grab a huge armful of mud, which he dragged out to sea with him to play with.

Out in the ocean, floating in the great waves, he played with the mud and sand to his heart's content. Then gradually, over the centuries, he began to miss his mother and father. One day he decided to go home. But as he stood up he realized he was lost. He couldn't go home! He would never see his family again!

The baby glacier sat down and cried, and his tears trickled down through the mud and sand. He cried and cried, until one day his mother heard him and came and found him. She lifted him up in her great glacier arms and carried him home, leaving the pile of mud and sand behind.

Now the baby glacier lives way up north again with his parents. We call his pile of mud and sand Nantucket. And the baby glacier's tears are still there under the mud and sand—so pure and clear that they supply all the drinking water for the people of Nantucket.

Kevin read the story over once, folded it up, and put it away. He didn't know what he would do with it—Sam was certainly too young to understand it yet—but writing it had satisfied some deep need. When the time was right, he would show it to Sheri.

CHAPTER 13

"How is he?" Mary asked Russell when he came home.

"Bad. They airlifted him to Mass General. Spinal cord might be injured."

"Oh, no!"

"I feel sick," Russell said. He sat down and bent forward, head in hands. "God, it's been one thing after another."

Mary came over and put her arms around him. Russell began to sob, with deep, wrenching shudders.

"Things aren't all bad," she said.

"They sure seem bad."

"You have the house. You have Sam and me."

"You've been pissed at me."

"We've all been under a lot of pressure."

"When will it end?" Russell looked at her so help-lessly, a wave of pity and love for him flowed through her.

"It will end, Russell. You're a good man. It will end."

He shook his head. "Sometimes it seems like everything's coming apart."

Mary was looking off into the distance. "Feel," she said. She pressed his hand to her abdomen. The new baby was stirring inside. Russell sat there quietly, feeling the flurry of tiny flutters, the occasional kicks that came heavy and sudden, like quick taps of a soft-headed hammer. Mary's skin, stretched tight and drumlike, thrummed with each blow. Russell thought Mary must be in pain. But with her hand next to his, she was gazing off into the distance with an expression of pleasurable reflection. She felt him watching and turned to him with a smile, and he bent over and kissed her on the forehead. Her skin was cool and dry and seemed somehow to promise the return of order and goodness to the world.

About nine that night, as Russell and Mary were drifting off to sleep, the phone rang. Russell made his way groggily out to the kitchen and answered it. It was Suzanne.

"Heather just told us," she said. "Do you know anything more about Roger?"

"They airlifted him to Mass General."

"So it's serious."

"It may be, Suzanne, I'm sorry to say."

"No one knows where Mike is," Suzanne said. She couldn't go on. Mary, who had pulled on her bathrobe and followed Russell out into the kitchen, took the phone from him.

"Suzanne, hi," she said. She heard Suzanne crying and said, "I'm coming over."

Suzanne was sitting at the kitchen table. When she let herself go limp in Mary's arms, Mary knew immediately that the distance Suzanne had been keeping between them had given way. Suzanne cried for several minutes while Mary held her. For her part, Mary no longer felt the need to talk or prove her caring. It was enough just to be there.

Frank, pacing about the house, nodded once from the doorway to the dining room and then disappeared. His lips were pressed tightly together, emphasizing the dimple on his chin. Mary had never before seen him look so stiff and frail, so old.

"He doesn't know what to do with himself," Suzanne said finally, nodding after Frank's departing figure. "Heather says Mike only started to fight to defend me from . . . from what people were saying."

Suzanne patted her eyes dry with a handkerchief. She sat down at the table, and Mary took a seat beside her.

"Heather is out looking for Mike now," Suzanne said. "She thinks she can convince him to go to the police on his own, before he's arrested."

They sat in silence, drinking tea, and later Frank came in and sat with them. He didn't speak except to ask if they wanted more tea. He brought it over and then retreated to a chair in the corner, where he sipped at a cup of coffee with a brooding, wounded air. Outside, it had begun to rain, and the wind was howling through the telephone lines.

The door opened, bringing in a rush of wind; a hooded figure stood in the doorway. It was Heather. She pushed back the hood and shook out her blond hair.

"No sign of him," she said.

Frank stood up. "Thanks anyway for looking, honey," he said. There was a note of apology in his voice.

"I was thinking, though. I didn't look out in Madaket," Heather went on, in her matter-of-fact way. "What if he took your boat?"

"Oh, Christ, he wouldn't do that, would he?" Frank said.

"The Hussey men do some pretty impulsive things," Heather said.

"That's enough of that," Frank snapped. "Do you understand? That's enough!"

"You want me to go look?" Heather asked coolly, ignoring her father's outburst.

"Naw, I'll call Milton. He lives right by the boatyard. He can go check for the boat."

"Okay," Heather said. She walked over to her mother and massaged her shoulders. Suzanne looked straight ahead, not responding.

Frank was on the phone.

"Hi, Milton. . . . No, worse and worse. Mike got himself in a fight at the shanty, and he's disappeared. There's some thought here that he took my boat. . . ."

Frank finished the call and paced around the kitchen, waiting for Milton to call back. In the warm yellow light from her small lamp, Suzanne's skin looked almost bronze. Her face was calm and resigned, register- ing no pain.

The phone rang again about ten minutes later.

"Yeah, that's the slip," Frank said. "It's gone? Thank you, Milton. . . . No, no reason to go out after him. Just have to sit tight and wait. . . . Sure, sure, if you want. I'm sort of outnumbered here," he added in a quieter voice, but loud enough for the others to hear.

"You were right," he told Heather as he hung up. "She's gone. Well, he won't get far in this storm. I forgot to fill the gas tanks today." He wheeled and walked out of the room.

"Frank, shouldn't we call the Coast Guard?" Suz- anne called after him.

"Those clowns! They'd only get lost themselves."

"Heather, you shouldn't speak like that to your

father," Suzanne said, after he was gone. She spoke firmly but without anger.

"I can't help my opinions," Heather said.

"Some opinions don't need to be expressed. You only hurt your father."

"So what?" The question hung in the air.

Mary got up to put on more water for tea. There was a knock on the door, and Milton came inside, wiping the water off his face.

"It's getting nasty out there," he said. "Where's Frank?"

"In the back," Mary said, assuming the role of hostess. "Tea or coffee?"

"Coffee," Milton said, rubbing his hands together. He accepted the coffee and looked from Suzanne to Heather. Suzanne's head was bent; perhaps she was sleeping. Heather was staring at the floor and biting her lip. "I'll go find Franky," Milton said.

Frank was downstairs in the shop, making a new door for the head of the stairs. He had laid out six tongue-in-groove boards and was ripping battens to screw onto the back. He nodded at Milton and kept right on working. Clouds of sawdust flew around him; the table-saw blade zinged through the wood, an arc of silver. Frank finished the last cut and turned off the saw. The brake engaged with a loud *clomp,* and the sawdust and noise dropped away.

"Hi, Franky," Milton said in his friendly, soda-bottle voice.

"Evening, Milton."

"Tough luck, huh, Franky?"

"Looks like I've screwed up all around."

"Feel outnumbered, you said."

"Yeah, I guess I'm persona non grata around here."

"It'll all work out."

"I don't know, Milton. I don't know. My own daughter is telling me to my face what a louse I am."

"Daughters take this sort of thing hard."

"Hell, she's the one who told me to hire the girl in the first place. But there's more. Now it seems I'm responsible for Mike's getting in a fight. Heather said he was defending his mother's honor."

"You couldn't help it."

"Hell, maybe it all is my fault. If I had stayed clear of that girl—"

"Franky, I gotta ask you something," Milton said, in a serious, careful voice. He was looking at the floor. He cleared his voice and went on. "Did you try and . . . run 'er aground?"

Frank looked at Milton, his eyes wide with surprise. For a second it almost looked as though he would smile, but then he was grimacing.

"Hell, no, Milton," he replied.

"You mean it just happened. The whole thing just happened by accident?" From his tone of voice he clearly hoped to receive an affirmative answer.

"Yep," Frank said. "Whole damn thing."

"Well, you know, in my book that makes a difference. It makes it better."

"Better?" Frank asked. "What's that got to do with it?"

"Well . . . everybody makes a mistake."

"Who made this mistake, huh? Me or her?"

"I think you both did, Franky."

"You know, the hell of it is, she's a nice girl," Frank said, placing one of the battens in position and screwing it down with a screw gun. "But nobody's going to believe it."

"I wouldn't worry about her if I was you," Milton said. "You have to think of Suzanne."

"Oh, I think of her. But I don't know what good it'll do."

"She has a big heart, Frank. She'll forgive you."

Frank looked over at Milton, and there was a change in his eyes. For the first time he looked steadily at Milton. Then he put down the screw gun.

"You know, that's the hell of it. I did wrong. What I should do is just apologize and get it over with. But I don't know if I can."

"Why not?"

"Christ, I don't know. I'm too damn proud or something. If I knew why, I'd be sitting in a shrink's chair somewhere with a diploma on the wall, not dredging the bottom of the harbor for scallops."

"Just tell Suzanne you love her, Franky. You made a mistake. She'll forgive you."

"It's gonna take an awful long time, if ever," Frank said. He shook his head.

"Don't forget how much you love her, Franky."

Frank turned away and stood in thought, looking at the wall.

Upstairs, there was a knock on the door, and Russell came inside, carrying a drowsy Sam. Russell's hair and beard were soaking wet.

"Russell! What are you doing here?" Mary said, standing up.

"We got lonely," he said, with a little smile.

Mary went over and took the baby. Sam rested his head on her shoulder and fell back into deep sleep. His plump mouth was slightly open, and his cheeks looked translucent in the kitchen light.

"Look how content he is!" Suzanne said.

Russell and Mary, only one year old as parents, couldn't help but beam, and their joy seemed to spread. The presence of a small child lightened the mood in the house. Suzanne held out her arms, and Mary handed Sam to her. With a practiced air, Suzanne laid him across her lap, resting his head on the padded arm of the chair. Sam stirred once and was still. Suzanne watched him, and the expression on her face grew almost peaceful.

"I have a friend," Suzanne said, in her soft, musical voice, "who asked me a little while ago, 'What's the most beautiful sight you ever saw?' And I thought about it, and I said, 'Dawn over Tuckernuck.'" Suzanne turned to Mary. "How would you have answered?"

Mary thought a moment.

"Probably the moors out by Polpis," she said. "One evening in October there was a beautiful sunset, and the hills were glowing in the light. We were about to go, when Russell said wait. And then the largest, roundest full moon I ever saw rose up over the hill. And the western sky was still orange, but the moon was all silver in the east." She sat silently, remembering the moment.

"Sort of like an orange Creamsicle," Russell added.

"How about you, Russell?" Suzanne asked.

"No question about it," Russell said. "A dredge full of Horseshed scallops." After the laughter, he said, "Or maybe our house, the day we finished framing it."

"Heather?" Suzanne asked.

"The dew on the grass in early morning, when I ride my bike," Heather said. "The way it sparkles." She was sitting on the floor, clasping her legs to her chest and resting her head on her knees.

Frank and Milton came up the stairs.

"Milton," Suzanne said. "We're talking about the most beautiful sight we've ever seen. What was yours?"

"The first time I saw the Concorde go overhead,"

Milton said. "A flame of silver. I couldn't believe my eyes." Spread-eagling his fingers, he pantomimed how it had looked.

"How about you, Frank?" Mary asked.

"The most beautiful sight I ever saw?" Frank repeated, and his face took on a thoughtful expression. The lines around his eyes softened. "My wife on our wedding day, coming down the aisle in white, with a wreath of wildflowers on her head." He looked down at the floor.

"But what did your friend say?" Mary asked Suzanne. Suzanne paused a moment, looking toward Frank. At first there was a flash of anger in her eyes; then something in her expression changed. She turned back to Mary.

"She said I had it all wrong. She said the most beautiful sight in the world was a sleeping baby, and if you can't see that, you've missed the whole point." She kissed Sam on the face and watched him stir softly.

They sat there into the early morning, drinking tea and talking, and a quiet acceptance fell over the group, bound together as they were by the sea and misfortune and love. Suzanne put Sam down on a bed in the back room, and when she returned, she took a seat beside Frank on the sofa. He put his arm around her, and she leaned her head on his shoulder and fell asleep.

When dawn came they were all sleeping, sprawled on the sofa and the chairs. Russell was on the floor at Mary's feet. Frank stirred first to put on water for coffee. Suzanne felt him move and joined him without speaking. He brushed against her once and she pulled away. As morning came the sight of Frank made her confused and unhappy again. She busied herself with breakfast.

The others woke up to the smell of eggs and bacon and coffee. Suzanne sat them down at the table and served them. Before he joined them, Russell called the hospital. There was no information on Roger; Russell left the phone number for the hospital to call back.

It was still blowing outside, though the rain had stopped.

"So, what's the plan, Cap?" Russell asked Frank.

"Plan?" Frank repeated. "Well, I think you should go out and get your scallops this morning. They ain't gonna wait around for you, and if you don't get 'em, others will."

Russell waved his arm. "I can miss a day," he said. "I'd rather help, if I can."

"Help how?" Frank asked.

"Help you find Mike."

"It's a big ocean out there," Frank said.

"Don't you think he went somewhere?" Russell asked.

"Sure. Somewhere. But where was that?" Frank asked.

Before Russell could answer, the phone rang, and he jumped up and answered it.

"No, I'm not Frank," he said. "I'll get him."

Frank took the phone.

"Hello," he said. "Oh, hello, Maude. What can I do for you? . . . Oh, you don't want to speak to me? Okay, here's Suzanne." He made a face and handed the phone to Suzanne.

Suzanne took the phone from him. Maude wanted to know why all the strange people were there and what was going on. Suzanne talked to her for several minutes, explaining what had happened.

"It's plain as punch where the boy went," Maude told her.

"Where?" Suzanne asked.

"To Tuckernuck, of course."

"Maybe you're right," Suzanne said.

"Of course I'm right. But tell me, dear, are you all right?"

"Getting there," Suzanne said. "I've thought of what you told me."

"Good. I'll let you go now. You go find that son of yours."

"All right," Suzanne said. She hung up the phone and announced to the others, "Maude says Mike has gone to Tuckernuck."

Russell slapped his knee. "Damn! I bet she's right!"

"He might have gone to Tuckernuck," Frank said, accenting the last syllable as he always did. "Yep, he might of."

"Let's go," Russell said.

Mary was carrying Sam into the room. She stopped and asked, "Where are you going?"

"To Tuckernuck," Russell said. "To get Mike."

"Not so fast," Frank told him. "It ain't going to be easy to get to Tuckernuck from town today. It's blowing out there something fierce. I'm not so sure your boat can handle the sound in weather like this."

"Sure, my tank can do it."

Frank nodded his head slowly and raised his eyebrows. "Okay, Russell. If you're sure she can handle it."

"No problem," Russell said.

"Your engine okay?"

"Engine's fine."

"Well, okay then."

"I'm coming," Suzanne said.

"Gonna be rough out there," Frank told her. "Six-, seven-foot seas."

"I want to go," she insisted.

Frank pursed his lips, folded his arms, nodded his head.

"Franky, you sure about this?" Milton asked. "It's gonna be bad in the sound. I could run my Whaler out from Madaket."

"It's okay, Milt," Frank said, picking up his coffee. His decision had been made, and he didn't want it questioned. "Even in Madaket harbor you'd need more boat today than a Whaler."

There was a knock at the door. Russell pulled it open—and found Kevin.

"Oh, hi, Kevin," he said. "I didn't get in touch with you this morning, did I?"

"I saw your truck here, so I thought I'd come over. What's up?"

"Got the morning off, Kevy." Russell told him what was going on.

"Okay," Kevin said. He spoke quietly to Russell for a minute more.

"I don't know, Kevy," Russell replied. "I'd better clear it with Mary."

"Okay. Any chance you'll want me later?"

"Naw. Just write the day off. Too rough today for scalloping anyway."

Milton stepped outside to sample the weather and Russell introduced them.

"Kevin's my culler. He's also a musician. Concert violinist," Russell said, with some pride in his voice.

The phone rang, and Russell ran inside.

Milton pulled Kevin aside. "Did Russell tell you what they're planning to do?"

"Yes."

"I'm worried about them. I'm going to go out from

Madaket in my Boston Whaler. Wouldn't hurt to have someone along. You want to come?"

"Sure," Kevin said. "Just give me a call when you're ready to go." He gave Milton his phone number.

There was a whoop from inside.

"That was the hospital," Russell shouted. "Roger is okay. His neck is gonna be okay, everything!"

CHAPTER 14

When Russell, Frank, and Suzanne came to the end
of the jetties and turned west toward Tuckernuck,
the wind was full in their faces. For the first time that
season it had a wicked wintry bite. Their cheeks and
noses were numb after a few seconds, though they
turned their heads from the spray that pounded over
the deck. It was too cold for Suzanne, so she sat down
in the bow, out of the wind and water, on an upturned
scallop box. Every few minutes she stood up and
scanned the sea for signs of her son. Frank stayed aft of
the culling board, with Russell.

Steep waves heaved and fell away around the boat
in a ceaseless succession of mountain ranges. Peering
intently ahead, Russell did his best to thread his way
through the valleys. He successfully avoided most of the
waves; they flopped languidly against the bow, sounding
like bags of sand tossed from a pickup truck. But occasionally a wave smashed across the gunwales with a
terrific force that made the boat shudder.

After one such huge wave struck them, Frank
glanced over at Russell with a questioning look.

"She's doing okay," Russell shouted, over the engine noise and the wind.

Frank raised his eyebrows and nodded.

Suzanne stood up and pointed toward something. Frank looked but shook his head at her. She looked again and sat down. Watching them, Russell knew all wasn't well between them. He wished he could help; he wished he could share the blissful, dreamy sensation he had now when he thought of Mary and Sam. Something inside him had let loose last night—some compulsion, some fear—and his family was close in his thoughts again. No matter what happened now, everything was all right.

The trip to Tuckernuck from the town harbor was roughly nine miles. For close to an hour, they continued along the northern shore of Nantucket, about a quarter of a mile out from shore. By the end of the hour, Russell could make out individual houses on Tuckernuck, on top of the hill. It was still impossible to see if a boat was anchored by the island.

But one thing was becoming increasingly clear: the wind was still rising and the seas were getting rougher. Had it been a west wind, the Tuckernuck shoals would have offered them protection as they approached. But because the wind was from the north, the waves came at them unobstructed from a thirty-mile stretch of open sea. One huge wave suddenly appeared above them and smashed across the deck, streaming over them and leaving three inches of water in the boat. Russell shook his head and tried to blink the salt water out of his eyes. Another wave caught them on the starboard and sent them lurching to the side. The boat tipped perilously and finally righted itself.

"Better head off nor'west." Frank shouted above the roar of wind and water. "Come back south later. You gotta take seas like these head on."

Russell adjusted their course more directly into the waves. The bow lifted and crashed down again and again. Suzanne crawled under the culling board and joined the others in the stern. She stood holding onto the board with both hands. Her face was white, and she didn't speak. She seemed mesmerized by the sight of the flying gear in the boat. Empty scallop boxes, an oar, an electric lantern slammed up and down with each wave: she watched their oscillation as though they defined some steady, unchanging point about which the universe was moving.

"I hope she's as strong as you say," Frank shouted.

Russell grimaced. He had never brought the boat into waves like this. They were so high now that when the boat fell into the valleys he couldn't see over the surrounding peaks: all he could see was the gray, threatening sky directly above them.

They continued to the northwest for about half an hour. With each wave Frank watched carefully, but he approved of the way Russell was steering and made no further comment. After half an hour they were still about seven miles from Tuckernuck, though it now lay to the southwest instead of the west. Nantucket was about four miles to their south and looked almost as far away as Tuckernuck.

"Bring her back sou'west?" Russell shouted.

Frank looked around and nodded. "Does she surf good?" he shouted.

"Guess we'll find out!" Russell said, with a small, wry grin.

"Bring 'er around fast!" Frank cautioned.

Russell brought the boat around to port. One wave caught them from the side, and he swung the boat around on it.

"Nice!" Frank exclaimed.

Then they were flying with the waves. A pattern quickly established itself. They would ride a wave for ten or fifteen yards, slip off it, and then the next wave would catch them. Russell was reminded of Saturday night, when he and Kevin went looking for Frank. That seemed weeks ago, not just three days.

It was much quieter this way, running before the waves. There was almost dead silence as they caught a swell. The noise came as they slipped off; the water seethed out from under them, and the motor raced momentarily as the stern rose and the prop pulled out of the water. Then the eerie quiet returned.

Frank nodded his head in satisfaction at the way Russell was maneuvering on the waves. They made good time, and in half an hour Tuckernuck was only a few miles away. Suzanne stood and scanned the water. Then she was pointing.

"There's the boat!" she shouted. A white boat was moored near the island.

"See it, honey?" Suzanne asked Frank. He shook his head. His eyes weren't good enough any more.

Suzanne bent over closer to him, put her arm around him, and pointed.

"Can you see now?" she asked. He shook his head no.

Suzanne's arm had stayed around him in the excitement of spotting the boat. In a moment she had forgotten the events of the past few days, and everything felt as it always had. But then, seconds later, the shock and disbelief and pain came back in successive waves. She looked over at his face—buried deep in the hood of his oiler—and wondered if she would ever be able to remember what he had done yet feel close to him at the same time.

She pulled away from him, then thought better of it and came over and took his hand. He looked at her; it was the first direct look they had exchanged in two days. One eye regarded her with a timid, curiously open glance; the other seemed distant and cold. But that was the way his eyes had always been; that was the way he had always been. A surge of love for him flowed through her, despite everything, and then she felt the pain again and turned away.

There was a tap on her shoulder.

"I see it," he said. She nodded, without looking over at him.

They were now about half a mile from Tuckernuck. Frank was eyeing the water in front of them and shaking his head. He seemed troubled about something. He raised his arms above his head and then lowered them.

"Something wrong, Cap?" Russell asked.

Frank didn't answer. He fell to his knees and rested his head against the culling board.

"Honey, what is it?" Suzanne asked, bending down next to him.

Frank shook his head. "I don't know. I feel like crap. Leg hurts like hell, for one thing."

Russell looked down at him with a concerned expression. "Should I turn back?" he asked.

"Hell, no," Frank said. "Take her in to Tuckernuck."

"I was relying on you to tell me where the shoals are. I might be able to tell in good weather, but not in a storm like this."

Frank shook his head again and waved his arm feebly.

Russell steered in silence for a few minutes. He was still heading before the wind, surfing on the waves. But as the boat slid off an especially large wave, it shuddered and paused for a moment before the next wave caught it and lifted it forward.

"Damn!" Russell shouted. "We've hit a shoal!" He swung the wheel hard to starboard. The boat struck a wave, rose, twisted, and fell at an angle. There was the sound of smashing, splintering wood. More quickly than Suzanne could register the events, the bow filled with water and began to sink. The stern slowly followed it down.

Russell yelled and slammed his fist on the gunwale.

Frank drew himself up on the culling board and glanced around.

"Oh, Christ, Russell," he said. "Now you've done it."

A wave rolled into the boat, with a lazy, powerful sweep. It left them standing up to their waists in frigid water. The water gave their legs a burning sensation.

"On the next wave, swim for the shoal," Frank said.

"Can you swim, honey?" Suzanne asked.

"Don't worry about me."

The wind blew away his words, and a new wave loomed over them. Without thinking, just reacting, Suzanne let herself go with it, as though she were body surfing. She was under, then she was above. She found herself surrounded by water, with another wave coming from behind. Without conscious thought, she yielded herself to that wave and the next and the next. Then the waves were breaking around her, and she found she could stand. She waded farther onto the shoal, where the water was only up to her knees. She looked around. Russell was about fifty yards to her left, shaking his head and flailing his arms. He had made it to the shoal too.

But Frank was nowhere to be seen.

"Frank!" she shouted. She waded back into the water. "Frank!"

Then she saw him—a yellow-gray mass crawling from the breakers no more than twenty yards away. She reached him just as a wave arrived, and she and Frank were hurled onto the shoal together. When she fought clear of the water he was lying beside her on the sand. His eyes were open; his arm moved; he was trying to speak, but she couldn't hear him. It seemed that the noise—the crashing of the waves, the fury of the wind—was draining the life from him.

Russell came running over through the foaming surf.

"Can you walk?" he asked her.

"I think so."

"We've got to get him to shore." Blue with cold, Russell bent over, hoisted Frank onto his shoulders, and staggered through the breakers toward shore. Suzanne followed him, moving forward on legs that had no feelings, on feet that felt like concrete, through water that stretched forever. The great wide world shrank to one object: keeping up with Russell and her husband as they receded down a long tunnel toward the distant horizon.

Russell staggered ahead of her onto the beach. Suzanne found herself beside them.

"Over there!" She pointed. "The boathouse!"

She fought her way into the wind toward the boathouse, about fifty yards up the shore. Russell came behind her, still carrying Frank, who held on with unconscious strength. Suzanne came to the door; it was unlocked. She pushed it open and went inside. She spread out some sails and they laid Frank down. He watched them through half-opened eyes.

"Help me get his clothes off him," she said. She pulled off his oilers and tried to unbutton his vest, but her fingers were too cold and numb to have any effect.

Russell stepped over and simply ripped the clothes off him, down to his underwear.

"Do the same to me, and wrap us up in the sail," she said. Russell did as he was told. Suzanne rolled into the arms of her husband, into a body as cold as winter sand. In the distance she still heard the crashing of waves, a thickening blanket of sound that grew and grew until it finally became one with her breathing.

Kevin was at home with Sheri, waiting for Milton's phone call. It was the first quiet morning they had spent together in a long time; they didn't discuss anything seriously, and both welcomed the relief. They simply listened to music and chatted.

"When is he going to call?" she asked, after a while.

"Any time. Will you come with us?"

"No, Kevin."

"Why not?"

"It will look like I'm barging in on them."

"You're the EMT."

"That's not fair, and you know it."

"Okay, I'm sorry."

Sheri was silent a minute. "The most important thing would be to take a two-way radio. If someone needs help, you'll have to contact the hospital some-how."

"I don't know if Milton has a radio. I don't even know how big his boat is."

"He should be able to borrow one from the fire station."

"I'll ask him about it when he calls."

The phone call came about ten o'clock.

"You still want to come?" the tenor voice inquired across the phone lines.

"Absolutely." Kevin asked Milton about a radio;

Milton thought it was a good idea and said he would stop by the fire station on the way.

Kevin put on his boots and oilers and waited. A few minutes later, Milton pulled up in front and tooted his horn.

"Well, goodbye," Kevin said. He took a step toward Sheri and stopped.

"Goodbye." Sheri watched as he climbed into the car. As they drove away, memories came flooding back, and she sat down on the floor and buried her head in her arms.

And then, for the first time, she understood her powerlessness with her father, and her need to exert her power over Frank. What she had been trying all along was to undo the past, but the past can never be changed.

Kevin and Milton rode out to Madaket in silence. They left behind the tall gray-shingled houses of Pleasant Street, followed Upper Main Street past the Civil War monument, and continued on Madaket road out through the moors, which seemed wild and unsettled in contrast with town. But skeletons of new houses were already rising in the gray hills, and here and there bright yellow shingles told the tale of another already completed home. They drove by the dump (recently renamed a landfill) and crossed the head of Long Pond, where a flock of swans had gathered for shelter. At Madaket they followed the turnoff for the Hither Creek Boat Yard.

Milton's Boston Whaler was docked at the boatyard. Sheets of water fell on the surface of the creek; the swamp grass was flattened by the gale. Struggling against the wind, they climbed into the Whaler and headed down Hither Creek, past the moored boats. The wind was so strong that several boats had come off their moorings and blown ashore.

Madaket is much closer to Tuckernuck than the town harbor, and normally the boat trip took about fifteen minutes. But today it would take three times that long, even though Madaket harbor was in the lee of the strong winds. As they came out of the creek and pushed their way into the harbor, large curling waves greeted them. The little boat pounded across the gray foaming water.

Slowly, they came closer to Tuckernuck.

As they rounded Eel Point and started across the small stretch of open water between the two islands, Kevin pointed at Tuckernuck and shouted. Frank's Sea Ox was bobbing in the shallows near shore.

"Mike's there!" Milton's voice sounded above the engine. "I wonder where the others are!" He opened the throttle as wide as it would go. The little boat leaped across the waves, which faded into black at the horizon. Spray poured over them, dripping down their oilers.

As they came closer, Kevin spotted something on the shoals a few hundred yards past the boat.

"Looks like a shipwreck!" he shouted.

"Oh, jeez!" Milton exclaimed. He steered in that direction.

They came closer to the wreck.

"Oh, jeez!" Milton exclaimed again. "Where the hell are they?"

"I don't know."

A wave crashed over them, another.

"I can't go any closer. I gotta bring her around."

"Think they made it to shore?"

"I don't know. I'm going in."

Milton steered in toward the beach. The Whaler slid up onto the sand.

"No sign of them," Milton said.

Kevin climbed onto shore and Milton clambered up after him.

"It's worth taking a look," Milton said. "Maybe they're here—somewhere."

They walked off along the beach in opposite directions. Kevin made his way up to the boathouse and opened the door. With disbelieving eyes, he saw Russell, Suzanne, and Frank.

"They're in here!" His voice carried across the wind to Milton. Milton came running up and looked inside. Frank and Suzanne were wrapped up in the sail; Russell was slumped down beside them. A quizzical grin was on his face; he tried to speak but couldn't.

"I'll call the hospital!" Milton said. He ran down toward the boat to get the radio.

"I'm going after some blankets!" Kevin yelled. "I'll be back in a minute," he told Russell, who looked up at him, still smiling dumbly. Kevin tore up the hill, following the path to the houses, and burst into the Hussey house. Mike, who had been slumbering by the wood stove, leaped to his feet.

"What's going on?" he exclaimed.

"Blankets!" Kevin said.

He ran into the bedroom and grabbed an armful of blankets.

Mike was following him. "What are you doing?" he asked.

"Your mom and dad had a wreck," Kevin said. "They're in the boathouse."

Mike stared in silence a moment. Then he opened a dresser drawer, pulled out some more blankets, and ran down the hill after Kevin.

Kevin came into the boathouse with the blankets.

Milton helped him open up the sail that was wrapped around Frank and Suzanne. Kevin was shocked to see the well-defined musculature of the older man's gaunt body; for an instant he felt a surge of revulsion which was all the stronger because it had taken him by surprise. He slipped some blankets under Frank and Suzanne and rolled them back up. They were both semiconscious. Frank's face looked almost saintlike in repose; Suzanne's eyes were shut, and her face had a gentle, peaceful expression.

Following Kevin's instructions, Milton already had Russell's wet clothes off him

"One of us has to strip and get in a blanket with him," Kevin said. He paused a second. "Hell, I'm his culler; I'll do it." He stripped and lay down on a blanket beside Russell. "Roll us up," he told Milton. He turned into Russell's large, cold embrace.

"Don't get any ideas, big fella," Kevin said.

Mike was watching all this from a few steps inside the door. He was pale and breathing heavily.

"Sit down, Mikey," Milton said. "Sit down."

Mike knelt down by his mother. He reached out and touched her hair.

"Oh, God, Mom," he said.

A helicopter shattered the silence. Milton went outside and waved to it. As it swooped in for a landing, it reminded Kevin of the brutal beauty of the swans he had seen over Tuckernuck a few nights earlier.

A man and a woman entered the boathouse, bearing a stretcher. They carried out first Suzanne, then Frank, then Russell. Then, almost before Kevin knew it, the helicopter took off. For a second the noise was deafening as the chopper rose and turned, but it pounded off into the distance, leaving behind the sweep of the wind and the crash of the waves.

Kevin pulled his clothes back on. He was suddenly cold and exhausted.

CHAPTER 15

Frank, Suzanne, and Russell were airlifted to Nantucket Cottage Hospital and later that day transferred by helicopter to Mass General, where they were put in intensive care and treated for hypothermia. All three survived. Frank remained in ICU longer; it appeared he had suffered a mild coronary. He was given stern lectures on smoking and decided on his second day in the hospital to give it up once and for all.

It was as though Nantucket had taken over an entire wing of the hospital. Roger had remained there a few days for observation and was given Russell as a roommate. Frank and Suzanne were put in a room together. The first thing Suzanne noticed when she became conscious was a large arrangement of baby roses on the table beside her bed. The card read, *With hopes for peaceful rest—Maude.* But rest for Suzanne turned out to be less peaceful than she might have wished. In the next several days there were many visitors—of course Mary and Sammy and Mike and Heather, but also Milton and Jack and Sam and many others who made the trip into Boston for the day.

Frank and Suzanne slept most of the non-visiting hours. It seemed they had no time alone, what with meals and medications and examinations by doctors. By the third day, Suzanne was growing uneasy. They had survived; they would be all right. The initial euphoria of survival was fading. But nothing had changed. How could she and Frank lie within five feet of each other, twenty-four hours a day, and not even mention it?

It was Frank who brought it up that night, after visiting hours were over. He patted his bed, asking her to sit down by him, and when she was seated he said, "You know, honey, I've been thinking a lot about Tuckernuck recently." He paused then, as he usually did after initiating a conversation.

"Yes?" It was up to him to go on.

"Umm-huh. I was awful confused then, after my mother died. I was some lucky you were willing to take me on."

Suzanne listened in silence, wondering what he was trying to get at.

"We did fill up that house, you know," he went on. "We've had a pretty good time of it. Speaking for myself, that is. I've had it a lot better than I deserve, being married to you."

Suzanne found herself starting to smile, despite everything. He was so boyish when he tried to be nice. She felt her smile broadening as he stumbled on, looking for the right words.

"Then of course I go and act like a jerk. I didn't intend to; I don't know how it happened. But I can tell you this: it had nothing to do with my feelings for you, and it will never—"

"Okay, Frank, that's enough," Suzanne said. She put her hand over his mouth; her smile caved in to laughter. Frank's face reddened. He looked up at her, with a

218

boyish, chastened expression on his face. She noticed there were new patches of white in his hair.

"Don't say any more," she told him. "Okay?" She knew her laughter was about to turn into sobs, but she shook her head and kept it under control.

She pulled her hand away from his mouth. Frank regarded her silently.

"You can't believe it was that easy, can you?" she asked.

"No," he said. "I can't."

"Well, don't get any further ideas."

"Don't worry, I won't." He raised his right hand.

"And don't be surprised if I act a little strange from time to time. I've still got feelings about all this."

"You do?" he asked. He was looking at her as though she were some wonderful, mysterious creature far beyond his comprehension.

"Umm-huh. I don't like what you did. I don't like it at all."

"I don't blame you."

"Enough said. Now go to sleep, you louse, and when you wake up I'll try and be civil."

"I'll go to sleep right now—this very minute," he said. He lay down and closed his eyes and pretended to snore. She bent over and kissed him on the cheek.

"How was she?" she whispered. "Nine and a half? Ten?"

"No score," he replied, without opening his eyes. He put his arms around her and pulled her down close to him. "Because you know, Suzanne, I could never love anyone the way I love you."

Heather was also a frequent visitor to the hospital, but she spent more time with her mother than with her father, and she remained cool toward him, despite his attempts to be friendly. One day Suzanne tried to talk to her about it.

"You know, things are all right between your father and me."

"I'm glad," she replied, in a noncommittal tone.

"I wish you weren't so distant with him. I know it hurts him."

"That's too bad." She left the room, and there was no sign from her afterward that her attitude toward Frank would change.

That evening, Mike appeared in the doorway to Roger and Russell's room.

"Well, well, looky who's here," Russell said.

"How you doing?" Mike asked. The wild, unfocused glare was gone from his eyes. He looked young and scared.

"About as good as you can expect from a drowned, frozen rat. How about yourself?"

"Not so bad. Hi, Roger."

"Mike, how are you." Roger's voice was cold.

"Not bad." Mike rubbed the side of his nose with his finger. "I was—ah, glad to hear you weren't hurt too bad."

"Yeah? So was I." Roger's habitual anger burned from his eyes as he spoke.

"I was pretty stoned."

"You're always pretty stoned."

Mike just stood there; Russell knew he didn't know what to say.

"Let's not be too hard on the guy, Roger," Russell said. "Mike, I think it's damn good of you to come in here and apologize. Is that what you're trying to do— apologize?"

"Yeah, that's what I'm trying to do," Mike said.

"Can you accept his apology?" Russell asked, turning to Roger.

Roger thought this over for a minute. "Yeah, okay," he finally said. "For a fee."

"What fee?" Mike asked.

"You gotta cull for me for a week. For free," he said.

Mike thought about this a minute. "Okay," he said.

"Shake on it," Russell told them. Mike walked slowly over to Roger's bed and held out his hand.

"Gawd, it's just like something out of the movies," Russell said, sniffing and pretending to cry. "I love it," he sobbed, in a fake falsetto voice.

"Oh, shut up," Roger told him.

While Russell remained in the hospital, Mary and Sam came to Boston to be near him. Fortunately, one of Mary's cousins lived in the city, only a few blocks from the hospital. Mary and Sam slept there and spent most of the day with Russell. While she sat and talked, Mary worked on her lightship baskets; she finished three during Russell's hospital stay. She was growing bigger daily; the joke around the hospital was that she would be the next Nantucketer to be admitted.

Sam soon made himself the darling of the floor. He walked about from room to room, saying his favorite words: "Dada," "Yoda," "fruck," and "cat." When his daddy was asleep, he visited Frank and Suzanne, and he quickly made many other friends as well.

Russell was like a little boy in the hospital—joking with the doctors and nurses, causing trouble whenever he could.

The only thing that bothered him was the thought of his boat—broken, in pieces, never to sail again. He didn't have enough money to buy another one, not with all the unpaid bills for the house and very little money coming in. But one morning, Mary came into the room with a big smile on her face. She handed him an envelope.

"What's this?" he asked.

"Open it."

It was the papers for a boat—the *Tuckernuck*.

"I don't get it," he said.

"They raised the money."

"Who?"

"The other scallopers. Some people in the community. I think Mrs. Miller made a contribution."

"I still don't get it."

"You have a new boat, you dummy."

He sat there a moment, in silence.

"Not a Sea Ox?" he said finally.

"No, but it's a Privateer—fiberglass. It's two years old, but Milton said it's in excellent shape. It has a culling board an a small outboard. It's all ready to go."

Russell shook his head, still not comprehending. Mary stood by with a quiet smile.

Back on Nantucket, Kevin immersed himself in scalloping. While the others were in the hospital, he and Milton went out each morning on Frank's Sea Ox, which they had brought back from Tuckernuck. They split some of the proceeds between them and put aside the rest for Russell and Frank. This had been Kevin's idea; Milton had discussed it with Frank and Russell in the hospital and gotten the go-ahead.

Kevin found himself enjoying his time on the water. It was late November and beautiful Indian summer weather, with warm, calm days. He learned things he had never dreamed he would do: how to set tows, how to haul in dredges. He fell into the life of a scalloper as he never had before, and the days passed in a rhythm that was almost musical. Rise before dawn, eat a hearty breakfast, drive out to Madaket and meet Milton, load the boxes into the boat, start up the motor, leave the dock at daybreak, steer clear of the shoals on the way to Tuckernuck, set the first tow, start up the donkey engine, haul in the dredges and dump them on the board, set the next tow, cull off the board—again and again and again. There was a beauty in this life, but only because he knew he was helping Russell and Frank, and only because he knew it would not be forever. In the back of his mind, he knew he would be leaving soon. But in the meantime, the life was strangely uplifting.

Problems remained. The major one was the distance Sheri was keeping from him. Ever since the day of the shipwreck, Sheri had been in a deep depression. For several days she ate nothing but saltines and beef broth, refusing to talk about her feelings. She wanted to be left alone, and after his efforts to reach her obviously made her feel worse, Kevin let her be.

The audition with the talent agency was only a few days away, but for several days Kevin had unconsciously been preparing himself to cancel it. He had slowly come to realize that what mattered to him most was being part of a human community, a group of people who care for things of beauty and pass them down to the next generation. The self-centered life of a concert artist would set him outside that community. For the time being, Kevin's community was Nantucket. But in the larger world, it included people like Professor Blatt, the wizened little teacher with a name like a trumpet blast, whose eyes lit up as he discussed the grandeur of Bach or the glory of Mozart.

The days passed quickly, and on the eve of his scheduled audition, Kevin called up the New York agent and canceled it. He felt no regret. He had toyed with the idea of saying he couldn't make the audition because he had to go out scalloping that day; but on further reflection he saw that such a ploy would make scalloping a fetish, a fad. Instead, he explained quite simply to the agent that he had decided to become a teacher. The agent heard him out and asked if he still might be interested in smaller chamber music performances. Kevin thought a moment and said yes. It was done.

Later that same evening, Kevin wrote a letter to Professor Blatt, asking if he could return to graduate school and to his position there as a teaching assistant.

Sheri remained completely inaccessible for the entire first week after the accident. But while she wouldn't talk to Kevin or go anywhere, she was thinking hard and long. Many of her thoughts were about Frank: how she had spoiled whatever chance there had been for pure, honest affection between them. But more and more, she found herself thinking about Suzanne.

It seemed to Sheri there was a spirit of beauty that shone through Suzanne and could only be loved: no other reaction was possible. This spirit was in everyone, but it was usually ignored, betrayed, trampled under.

It seemed to Sheri that most people must have a heart like Suzanne's. It could be seen in the way they reacted to her, in the way they became kinder and truer around her. Suzanne could not light a fire that did not already exist. But at the same time, the goodness within would remain useless unless it was expressed. Somehow people had to cast away their selfish needs and act out of love.

There Sheri's thoughts stopped. Her loneliness took the form of these abstract, well-intentioned insights— but she made no move outward. With Kevin she remained distant, not even thanking him for respecting her need for solitude.

At the end of the week she had a phone call. She recognized the voice immediately.

"Are you going to visit me, or am I going to have to get out of my sickbed in search of you?"

"Aunt Maude!"

"Well?"

"I'll . . . I'll come right over."

For the first time in a week, Sheri put on her coat and went outside. She walked over to Maude's house and knocked on the door. The nurse let her in.

Maude was sitting in the living room, wrapped in blankets. As soon as she came in, Sheri saw her aunt's condition was worsening and she wished she had come to visit sooner. She took Maude's hands and bent over and kissed her on the cheek.

"You look terrible," Maude told her, in her low, gravelly voice.

"I'm all right. More important, how are you?"

"I'm slipping. It can't be helped."

"Is there anything I can get you?"

"Just sit with me, child."

Maude's face was pale as paper, and her eyes looked yellow in the dim light. She gazed gloomily at the floor, her face registering no emotion. She sat in silence for several minutes. Then, in a quiet voice, she said, "As you near the end, you think of beginnings. Did I ever tell you about Rebecca?"

"She was your daughter," Sheri said.

"Did I ever show you her picture?"

"Long ago, perhaps, when I was too young to remember."

"Get that album for me that's on the bookcase."

Sheri brought an old leather-bound album and laid it in Maude's lap.

"Open it to the first page."

Sheri did as she was told. The picture was of a blond little girl—all smiles and vitality—sitting in a bathtub with a toy boat.

"She's so cute!" Sheri said.

"That was taken a few days before she died."

"But she looks so healthy!"

"She caught a fever. It took everyone by surprise. To this day, the news of her death is still sinking in. I still can't believe it."

Sheri placed her hand on top of her great-aunt's. Maude looked up at her.

"Life is to be lived, Sheri. Don't waste yourself on regret. Learn your lessons and go on."

Sheri turned her head away and looked at the yellowing floor.

"Now I'm tiring," Maude said. "This is probably my last day at home. Come see me in the hospital."

"I will, aunt," Sheri said. She bent and kissed her aunt's cheek again. Then she turned and walked home through the gathering dusk.

Sheri visited Maude each day in the hospital from then on. They talked little; she sat quietly near Maude and sometimes read to her. She looked forward to seeing her great-aunt; it was the one thing she enjoyed now. With Kevin she was still distant, and in her walks to and from the hospital she walked with her head down, as though she had no right to look about or exchange greetings with anyone.

But a few days later, Sheri received an unexpected visitor. It was two days before Thanksgiving, and Russell and Mary and Sam had come home from the hospital.

226

That afternoon, Mary came over to the house on Pleasant Street and struck the solid brass knocker three times.

Sheri opened the door, washed-out and thin from her days spent inside and not eating.

"Come in," she said. "Kevin is still out scalloping," she added, as though she thought Mary's real reason for coming was to see him.

Mary sat down on a sofa in the living room, across from Sheri, who barricaded herself in a high-armed chair.

"Are you all right?" Mary asked

"Yes. Why?"

"You look as if you haven't slept in days."

"I haven't."

"Why ever not?"

Sheri just shook her head. "Why have you come?" she asked.

"I thought you would know. I've come to thank you and Kevin."

"I wasn't there."

"It was your idea to bring the radio."

"How did you know that?"

"Milton told me."

"Island life." Sheri sat silently for a moment, her mouth pulled taut. "It's hard for me to imagine what Suzanne must feel," she said. "And to think what they went through because of me."

Mary came over closer to Sheri. "Do you think you're the first person in the world to make a mistake?" she asked.

"Of course not."

"Do you really think the world is so small that you could destroy it?"

"Not the whole world. But someone's world." Sheri turned her head away. Her eyes had filled with tears.

She realized as she spoke how absurd she must appear, and yet she couldn't help herself.

Mary watched her in silence a moment, and went on. "You said something about how much everyone suffered because of you. What did you mean?"

"They were all out in the storm."

"Do you really think that was because of you?"

"Not directly, but indirectly."

"I wish you could see how wrong you are. They weren't there because of you."

"Yes, they were, at least indirectly," Sheri repeated.

"They weren't. That's where you're wrong. Russell was there because he loves Frank and wanted to help him. You had nothing to do with that. Suzanne was there because Mike is going through a difficult period. You didn't make her son the way he is. And you didn't make her husband the way he is, for that matter."

Sheri had stopped crying and was listening to what Mary said.

"And if you think you've ruined their lives, think again. Frank and Suzanne are happier now than I've ever seen them."

"May I get you something to drink?" Sheri asked. "Some tea?"

"I'd love some."

A few hours later, when Kevin came home, Sheri came to the door to greet him. She looked at him with a bemused, slightly ironic expression, and then she slipped her arms around him and gave him a quick kiss.

They didn't talk about anything in particular; they had a quiet, peaceful dinner. Afterward, he told her, "I have something I want you to read."

"What?" she asked.

Without replying, he walked out of the room and came back with a folded sheet of paper.

"Just read it," he said. "It's a children's story I wrote."

Sheri sat down and read it over. She turned to him with a puzzled expression.

"I like it," she said. "But why did you give it to me now?"

"I don't know," he replied. "It has something to do with a way of being. A way I want to be."

"Covered with mud?"

"Learning to care for children, to pass something on to them." He walked over to the window and looked out at the night sky. Orion the archer was low in the east.

Sheri was silent a moment. "I'm glad you've been thinking about the future," she said. "It makes a lot more sense than what I've been doing."

"Mulling over the past?"

"Yes."

"What about?"

"You know. How the past can't be changed."

"It can't. You just have to let it be."

He came up to her and kissed her on the forehead. "There's the future too," he said.

"We have lots of time to talk about that," Sheri replied. And Kevin realized then that she still needed in some way to keep herself separate.

Sheri wore her headscarf two more days, until Thanksgiving evening, when they finally had the conversation that all their thoughts and silences had been leading toward.

"Do you know that you missed your audition?" she asked him one evening.

"Umm-huh."

"Are you going to reschedule it?"

"No."

"Why not?"

"I want to go back to school. I want to teach."

She remained silent for a minute, as the import of his words sank in.

"When are you going to leave?" she asked.

"If I can get in for the second semester, I'll go then."

"Middle of January."

"Yes."

"Scalloping will be winding down by then."

"That's right."

They were both silent.

"Will you come back with me?" he asked.

She walked over to him, took his hands, and kissed him. "You've changed, Kevin. I like what I see. I hope I can keep up with you."

"You're fine just as you are."

She kissed him again. "The answer to your question is yes," she said.

He reached behind her head and untied the scarf and pulled down her long, dark glorious hair. That night they made love, for the first time in several weeks, and as they fell asleep afterward they both felt surrounded by happiness.

CHAPTER 16

The next few weeks passed quickly. Kevin went out scalloping again with Russell—in his new boat the *Tuckernuck*, which was his pride and joy. Kevin and Russell worked as equal partners now: they both stood aft of the culling board, and each of them hauled in one side. After a few weeks' extra rest, Frank started going out again, with Suzanne as his culler. Both boats worked out near Tuckernuck for the rest of the season.

Kevin and Russell were both in lighthearted moods their last month together; they took pleasure in their daily ritual. Russell came over to pick up Kevin at six each morning; it was pitch dark then as the days grew shorter. They worked hard all morning, looking forward to their lunchtime break. Then, as the other crews stopped a few minutes for a quick sandwich, Russell and Kevin made an elaborate production of their meal, piling fruit, pieces of chicken, sandwiches, cans of juice, and pieces of cake onto the culling board. About twenty other boats were working Tuckernuck shoal by this time, and Kevin and Russell took great delight in the reactions they got from the other scallopers.

One warm, calm, foggy day in early December, their unlikely friendship culminated in a display the likes of which had never before been seen in the scallop fleet. At noon they carefully washed off the culling board, and then they both ducked down out of sight. The boat drifted into a bank of glaring white fog which was hovering close to the water; it was just now beginning to lift. They were lost from sight for several minutes. When they finally emerged from the fog, Kevin was in a fine gray suit and Russell was in a black tux, with bright red suspenders that Kevin had given him as a get-well present. They spread a white tablecloth over the board and brought out bottles of wine, wheels of cheese, a bowl of oranges, and a whole chicken, roasted. Then they pulled up two empty scallop boxes, upside down, and sat and feasted. The sun came out, as though on cue. The other boats came over to observe. There was much shaking of heads and sarcastic comments. Roger, who was scalloping alone again (he and Mike had parted company after the agreed-on week with no love lost), was most vocal of all.

"You guys are really weird," he said.

"You're just jealous," Russell told him.

"Did you have those clothes on underneath your oilers all morning?"

"Naw, brought 'em in a sack."

"How long is this meal gonna last? All afternoon?"

"Who knows?" Kevin said. "We've apparently come to a cull-de-sack."

"Get out of here!" Russell told him. "No more of your lousy jokes."

"Lousy? Lousy?" Kevin protested.

"You must be really unhappy," Russell told him.

"Me unhappy?"

"You said humor comes from being unhappy."

"I've changed my mind."

"God, what a bunch of turkeys! Why don't you put

on an act for the tourists? They're all coming back this weekend for the Christmas stroll. You guys would be a big hit." Roger waved a hand at them and putted off in disgust.

A few minutes later, the strains of a solo violin echoed across Tuckernuck bay.

Main Street in downtown Nantucket had begun transforming itself in the early days of December. Christmas trees, gaily decorated by schoolchildren and various groups and organizations, lined both sides of the street, and lights and wreaths festooned the streetlamps and shopfronts. The Christmas Stroll, which had started off a few years earlier as a purely local expression of thanks by shopkeepers to townspeople, had rapidly grown into the largest single occasion for off-islanders to visit Nantucket. Some shops were known to do more business on that day than during the entire month of June; it was impossible to get dinner reservations for Saturday night unless they were made weeks ahead. At the same time that the Stroll was becoming a tourist event, it still remained a highlight of the Christmas season for the island children, who loved the crowds and the lights and the excitement and, most of all, the chance to meet Santa Claus, who always arrived in his sleigh Saturday afternoon to start off the celebration.

This year the warm weather of early December continued right into Stroll weekend, and by midafternoon Main Street was filled with streams of shoppers and islanders. A large crowd had gathered in front of the Hub gift store, where four men in top hats and long tails were singing Christmas carols. They sang three numbers and then ducked away, despite loud applause and shouts for more. As they made their way up Main

Street toward the Pacific Bank, it seemed that theirs were the only glum faces in the entire town.

"Oh, cheer up, guys," Jack was saying to the others. "Get in the Christmas spirit."

"Keep it to yourself," Sammy came back. "God, I feel like an idiot. I wish I was invisible or something."

"Aw, it doesn't hurt you," Jack told him. "Besides, it's good for the local merchants."

"It's just so damn fake. All these tourists think this is how we really live on Nantucket. Whale boats and top hats and all that crap."

"Well, we do have a special way of life out here. It may not be top hats, but it is different from what they're used to, and this lets them know it," Jack argued.

"What do you think of all this, Franky?" Milton asked. Frank was lagging slightly behind. The others stopped in front of Brock's Insurance, looking at the window display of a miniature town with a real working train.

"Me? I'm just glad to be here," Frank said. "Hell, I ain't so picky anymore."

He stopped and waved to Russell, who was standing nearby with little Sam in his arms, waiting in a line that led up the steps to the bank.

"What the hell you doing? They giving out money in there?" Frank shouted over.

"Naw, Santa's inside," Russell replied, grinning. "I want this little guy to see Santa."

"How's the little woman?"

"Not so little. Any day now, we'll have another one."

"Come on, Frank," Jack called back to him. "We're due at the J.C. house in three minutes."

"Gotta run," Frank told Russell. "See you soon."

A few minutes later, the quartet took its position

234

on the front steps of the Jared Coffin inn and launched into their four-part arrangement of "Hark the Herald Angels Sing." As they finished, Frank noticed Kevin and Sheri, arm and arm, walking past on their way to dinner at the Brotherhood. Sheri didn't look up, and for his part he turned quickly away and gave the pitches for the next carol.

Early Monday morning, Kevin received a phone call.

"I guess we won't be going out today, Kevy," Russell said.

"It happened?"

"It happened. A girl this time. A real beauty."

"Does she have a name?"

"Not yet. I thought we had one, but Mary and Suzanne are talking it over right now, and it may change."

"Everything go well?"

"Beautiful. Mary handled everything so well. I tell you, Kevy, birth is even better the second time around—no fears. It's just unbelievable."

"Hey, Russell, congratulations."

Later in the day, everyone learned that the baby's name was Maude Mary O'Grady. Mary had wanted to name the baby after Suzanne, but after talking to her she yielded to Suzanne's wishes and named the child for Maude Miller, who was just down the hall in the tiny Nantucket hospital.

That evening, Mary brought little Maude into Maude Miller's room. Little Maude was wearing a little cap and a cloth sacque. Her pale, pink face was all squinched up; she was fast asleep in Mary's arms. Maude Miller sat up in her bed. No expression registered on her face except for a sudden gleam of attention in her eyes.

"Give her to me," she said, in her deep, low voice. Very carefully, Mary handed her the baby. Maude held her tight to her chest with all that remained of her strength.

"You didn't have to do this," she told Mary. She looked down at the baby. "So young, so precious." For several minutes she stared intently at little Maude's face. The baby stirred in her sleep; the corners of her mouth lifted.

"She's smiling for you," Mary said.

"Don't be ridiculous; she has gas," Maude said. She held the baby a few minutes longer, in silence. Although her face was blank, Mary knew she was thinking hard about something.

The minutes ticked on.

"Shall I take her?" Mary reached toward the baby.

"No. I won't give her up," Maude said.

Mary took a step back.

A nurse appeared in the doorway.

"Hi, Maude. It's time to get the little one back to the nursery," she said.

"No." Maude said. "I've got her, and I won't give her up."

She turned her head away; there was a stubborn set to her jaw. Mary and the nurse exchanged a look. The nurse went out and came back in with Suzanne a few minutes later.

"Hi, Maude," Suzanne said.

"No," Maude said, shaking her head. She tightened her grip on the infant.

Finally Maude turned back toward them.

"All right," she said.

Mary walked over to Maude and carefully took the

baby from her. Little Maude stirred and raised tiny dimpled fists.

"Good night, Maude."

Wordlessly, Maude watched them leave, with vivid, glittering eyes.

Suzanne came back later and sat down by Maude's bed and took her hand.

"Damn it, Suzanne, it's harder than you'd think," Maude said.

"I know it is."

"You know, I still think of my little Rebecca. She'd be fifty years old next week. Can you believe it? Forty-seven years since I saw her, and I still think of her constantly."

"Of course you do."

"So here I am, dying childless. Not a damn trace left of me."

"Don't be silly. There are traces everywhere."

Maude waved her hand. "Oh, if it's names you mean—"

"It's not just names, and you know it."

Maude looked at Suzanne. "Good," she said. "I like to see you assert yourself." Then, suddenly, she seemed to grow tired. Her head nodded, and she fell into a peaceful sleep. Suzanne stayed with her awhile, watching the slow rise and fall of her breast. Then she bent down, kissed Maude's hand, and left the room. As she came to the door she met Sheri, who bowed her head and allowed Suzanne to pass. Suzanne paused a moment, looking at her, and then walked on.

Late that night Maude passed away. It soon became public knowledge that she had left a large gift to South Church, as seed money for the restoration fund.

Sheri found herself in charge of the funeral arrangements. Maude had left a note in which she asked to be cremated and designated the type of headstone she wanted. The note concluded:

I'm leaving a considerable sum to the church for renovation. It's my way of helping to preserve a special place. Nantucket will change—be more and more developed and carved up—but maybe, if enough special places can be saved, all will not be lost. Don't get lumpy about this service; it's just a natural part of life. And one more thing—I don't want any dreary organ music. I want the service to feel like spring. Ask the barbershop quartet to sing me one last song—I've already talked to Frank about this.

The morning of the funeral was gray, chilly and windy. A group of seventy or eighty people gathered in the front of the unheated church. The minister came out and gave a short talk about Maude—how she loved children and flowers and music, how the truth of her having lived remained, though she had passed on.

Then the quartet stood up and slowly made their way to the front of the church, near the trompe l'oeil columns. They lined up, looking somewhat bemused; Frank kept craning his head as though his collar were too tight. The song began. It was "Aura Lee." The first few chords were shaky and off-key, but as they went on it quietly fell into place. Sheri looked down at her hands and listened as the fresh, clean, masculine harmonies echoed beneath the dome of the church. The last chord mingled with solid tones of the church bell, striking noon.

*   *   *

As the end of December approached, Kevin and Sheri thought more and more about their return to Boston. Sheri was accepted into a graduate program in art at Boston University beginning in January. Meanwhile, Kevin received a short note from Professor Blatt.

Dear Kevin,

So glad to read of your decision to return. Of course you can start again in January. Much work to be done.

Have you really been scalloping? I'm allergic to shellfish myself, but I don't doubt that they serve some larger purpose in the universe. I can certainly understand why you might prefer shells to scales—major, minor, or fishy. And scalloping seems to have led you to the right decision. I still don't understand why you had to go to Nantucket to come to it, but look forward to discussing it with you upon your return.

Best
Prof B.

During all this time, Sheri had not talked to Frank. But one day when she went into Mitchell's Book Corner, looking for a Christmas present for Kevin, she saw Frank standing in the nonfiction aisle, touching his chin with his hand and looking puzzled. He had on the gray wool shirt he had always worn under his oilers.

Sheri's first impulse was to avoid him, but he turned and saw her, and their eyes met.

"Hi," she said, feeling herself smiling nervously.

"Hi, Sheri," he replied. His greeting was cordial; there was none of the distance in it that she had feared. He was wearing his winter cap pulled down low over his face; it make him look older than she remembered him. "You having a good winter?"

"Pretty good."

"I'm looking for a present for Heather, but I can't come up with anything. Any ideas?"

"You should buy her an art book," Sheri said.

"Oh. Yeah. Of course," Frank said. "What sort of art book?"

Sheri took him over and showed him some choices. He picked out a book of lithographs by a Nantucket artist.

"Sold," he said. He made a motion as if to go over to the sales counter.

"How have you been?" Sheri asked.

"Not too bad."

"You're not pushing yourself too hard?"

"Oh, no," he said. "Naw, I don't do that anymore. If we don't get 'em by noon, we come in."

She looked up—she felt it was for the last time—and was swept by the old flush of feeling for him as she saw his golden brown eyes. They looked the same color in the diffuse light.

"Kevin and I are leaving next week. On Christmas Eve."

"Back to Boston?"

"Umm-hum."

"Well, I wish you luck." Frank winked at her and turned to go.

"Frank," she called after him.

He turned back.

"Thanks for letting me be your culler."

"We had fun," he told her. She smiled, and he returned her smile; then, nodding his head, he turned away. A minute later, forgetting why she had come in, she walked out the door. She floated outside into the

240

cold December air, and as she made her way up Orange Street past the church, she had a sense that the world had returned to its rightful orbit.

Sheri and Kevin were leaving on the early boat the day before Christmas. They carried their belongings down to Steamship Wharf and bought tickets for the trip to Hyannis. It was just before dawn, a time they both knew well; the docks and boats and shoreline and water were beginning to take shape out of the darkness. Dockworkers shouted to each other; lights glimmered off the water. The great steel door of the boat swung open.

They put their suitcases on the luggage cart in the parking lot and waited to board the boat. It was six o'clock.

Just as the boat horn blew, announcing it was time to board, a figure emerged from the gray dusk and came up to Sheri.

"This is for you," a soft, musical voice said. Sheri looked up, knowing who it must be. Suzanne's face was before her, small and gentle in the darkness.

"I never thanked you both for . . . for the rescue. Please accept this," Suzanne said.

Sheri took the package from Suzanne. "Thank you," she said, too startled to say anything else.

Suzanne took a step back, as though unsure of what to do, and Sheri understood how much effort this must be costing her.

The boat blew three blasts from its horn.

"We'd better hurry or we'll miss the boat," Kevin said. "Thanks so much, Suzanne." He bent over and kissed her on the cheek. Sheri found herself shaking Suzanne's soft, firm hand. Then Kevin took her by the arm and walked her onto the boat.

Once they were seated, Sheri opened the box. Folded neatly inside was a long woolen scarf. Sheri lifted it out and draped it across her lap. It was spun from the soft browns and grays that she had come to love in the Nantucket autumn; it warmed her to look at them again.

"Isn't it beautiful," Kevin said. He put his arm around her and glanced up at her.

Holding the scarf in her lap, Sheri was gazing out the window. The steamship had pulled even with the Horseshed; the area they had fished in November was covered now with a thin layer of ice that rose and fell with the wake. Her eyes lingered there, then turned back toward town, which was already slipping off into the distance. In the clear dawn the hillside glowed faintly with a hue like ivory.

Sheri turned and looked full at Kevin, and her dark eyes searched his. She was remembering, and doubting, and wondering about the future; he allowed her to look without turning away.

Her gaze turned back to the town, as they steamed past the jetties and pulled clear, leaving Nantucket behind. It was impossible to distinguish individual houses now. But high above the rooftops, the golden dome of South Church glistened in a burst of sunlight.

Sheri wrapped the scarf around her shoulders and leaned over against Kevin.

"Let's get this show on the road," she said, smiling and reaching up to pull off his glasses.